MW00942815

PRAISE FOR TRIAL BY TWELVE:

"A satisfying novel, where plot, characters and setting blend into a compelling read. Heather Day Gilbert knows how to keep readers turning pages. Tess is one of those rare-to-me characters I'd like to have as a real-life friend."~**Janet Sketchley,** author of the *Redemption's Edge* series

"*Trial by Twelve* confirms Tess Spencer, the Glock-toting mountain mama of Buckneck, West Virginia, as one of my favorite amateur sleuths and Heather Day Gilbert as a first-rate mystery writer. This second book in Gilbert's *Murder in the Mountains* series ups the ante on the first: the stakes are higher, the tension runs deeper. Best of all, Gilbert kept me guessing until the end."~**Karin Kaufman**, author of the *Anna Denning* mystery series

"Heather Gilbert brings a fresh new voice to the mystery genre. I love the spunky Tess Spencer and her small town values. The first two books of this series are filled with plenty of suspense and the kind of characters that keep me coming back for more."~**Ron Estrada,** author of *Now I Knew You*

OTHER BOOKS BY HEATHER DAY
GILBERT:

Miranda Warning, Book One in *A Murder in
the Mountains Series*

God's Daughter, Book One in the *Vikings of
the New World Saga*

*Indie Publishing Handbook: Four Key
Elements for the Self-Publisher*

TRIAL BY TWELVE

A MURDER IN THE MOUNTAINS NOVEL
2

HEATHER DAY GILBERT

TRIAL BY TWELVE
BY: HEATHER DAY GILBERT

Copyright 2015 Heather Day Gilbert

ISBN-13: 978-1511740494
ISBN-10: 1511740493

Cover Design by Jenny Zemanek of Seedlings Design
Studio
Published by WoodHaven Press

Series: Gilbert, Heather Day. A Murder in the
Mountains series; 2
Subject: Detective and Mystery Stories; Genre:
Mystery Fiction

Author Information:
http://www.heatherdaygilbert.com

Author Newsletter:
http://heatherdaygilbert.com/newsletter-signup/

~*~

Dedicated to my brothers, Jon and Stefan
Computer whisperers, supportive readers, and
always ready to share your time—
I may be the shortest, but I'll always be your
protective big sis.

~*~

"It is better to be tried by twelve than carried out by six."

~*~

1

~*~

These letters may be hard for you to read, but someday you will ask who your father was. I have to explain why things turned out this way.

I didn't want a child. Your mother did, and I did whatever she wanted. I'm sorry to say but the woman is a shrew. I know that only begins to explain things, and it's not an excuse. But she drives me to the brink. I look in your eyes and I see some spark of me, and that's the spark I want to keep alive. When you turn sixteen, I hope to take you on a long-distance hunting trip, to understand why I need to get away periodically.

In life, we have chances for freedom. These trips are mine, and maybe someday they will be yours. "Follow your bliss" is the way of Buddha, and it's what I've committed to doing...for both of us.

~*~

Every day I have the same lunch: a tuna sandwich with lettuce and tomato on wheat. By the time I get to it, the lettuce and tomato have sufficiently sogged up the bread. I add to that a bag of sour cream & onion chips and a Cherry Coke from the vending machine, then throw any notion of healthiness to the four winds.

"You pregnant again?" Charlotte peers over the appointment desk at the Crystal Mountain Spa, where I've laid out all my food items.

"Nope...you have a problem with my menu?" I wink up at Charlotte, and she flutters her exotic eyelashes, two kisses of coal dust sweeping her high cheekbones.

"No judgments from me, Tess." She motions to her own lunch: a bag from Wendy's that doubtless contains a cheeseburger, fries, and chocolate Frosty.

I shove my lunch back in my tote. "Hey, let's go outside today. A breeze in July—not often we get weather like this."

She nods and stalk-walks to the side door, her long-legged gait the opposite of my own. My dear husband Thomas has informed me that I can't walk without natural hip action. The more I slow to adjust my walk, the more my hips determine to swing of their own accord.

"Deep thoughts?" Charlotte holds the door until I reach the stone-paved porch that encircles the log cabin-style spa.

"Not particularly."

"Good. Let's keep it light. My mom...it's hard seeing her that way."

Miranda Michaels, Charlotte's mother, is one of my best friends. Her insight helped me stop a killer a couple winters ago. But since then, she's had another heart attack and her health has rapidly deteriorated. And now a private nurse stays with her round the clock. We all know it's a matter of time.

Thank goodness Charlotte took a one-year leave of absence from teaching pottery at West Virginia University. She's camped out in Miranda's old house, which has shaped up nicely with more than a little elbow grease. Having Charlotte nearby has only cemented our friendship. I dread the day she decides to return to Morgantown.

When the sun hits our faces, Charlotte bursts into her customary three sneezes. Not one, not two, but always three sneezes for the sun. I snicker.

"I have no clue why you find that so funny." She curls into a faux leather chair. It's nothing but class for the Crystal Mountain Spa.

"Because you're literally allergic to sunlight, that's why." I perch on the stone wall, so I can better observe any wildlife in the ferny forest just beyond. "But getting back to your mom...does she know who you are?"

"Not anymore. But funny thing: she was calling for Mira Brooke the other day. She knows..."

Charlotte's voice cracks and I look back to the woods, knowing we're both on emotionally fragile ground. Miranda stayed lucid enough to understand Thomas and I named our firstborn daughter, *Miranda Brooke*, after her last June. We call her Mira Brooke. I take comfort that Miranda was able to hold her namesake in her thin arms at least three times before she lost her strength. But no amount of hoping can restore the *Grande Dame* to full health now.

The spa masseuse, Teeny, peers out the door at us. "How you doing, Charlotte?"

Teeny is a man with a wildly inappropriate nickname. He looks more like someone who should try out for the Mr. World contest. But he answers to nothing but *Teeny*. He also has a burning crush on Charlotte that will never in this universe be reciprocated.

"Doing good." Charlotte angles her legs and body away from Teeny, a clear sign he needs to give up.

He doesn't take the hint. "Your muscles feeling tight? I'll give you fifty percent off a half-hour neck and back massage."

His deep-set eyes fixate on her, as if he's unaware his co-worker is sitting right here.

I clear my throat, dropping the final scrap of tuna sandwich in my bag. "Pretty sure Dani said you shouldn't do that, Teeny."

He lumbers out on the patio toward me, like a Saint Bernard noticing a rabbit. "Do what?"

Our boss, Dani Gibson, has made it very clear that Teeny can't cut discounts or hit on possible clients. Sadly, Teeny is the best masseuse around and he can get away with anything he likes.

"That. What you just did. With Charlotte."

He wags his head back and forth slowly, like a pendulum. A new thought hits him.

"Tess, did you see the backhoes? They drove in this morning. Out back."

I feel like I'm talking to my brother-in-law Petey, who's only fourteen. "No—why are there backhoes here, Teeny?"

"Dani wants a pool. I mean we have the indoor pool but it's time for an outdoor one, she said. They were digging this morning before you came but they stopped early."

He shakes his head, befuddled, and heads back to his massage room. Apparently he has radar for when Charlotte enters the building, because he rarely emerges any other time.

Charlotte stands, peering around the side of the patio. "Another pool? Where does your boss get her money?"

"Well, you know this spa charges top dollar. I'd say there's not another spa like this in three counties."

"Yeah, full of incense and crystals...it's a wonder anyone from Buckneck darkens the door."

I secretly agree with Charlotte. The success of Dani's spa is astonishing, as no one in our small town seems inclined to get their energies balanced or to catch up on the latest in chakras. The only thing I can figure is that Dani snagged the best and brightest masseuse, hairdressers, and nail technicians for miles around. I only took the job because I wanted part-time hours and I've been a receptionist before. Correction: *Administrative Assistant.*

We polish off our food in the sunlit, hazy silence. This is what I love about Charlotte: we don't have to talk. We can just *be.*

A clattering of high heels sounds on the flagstones. Dani, an enigmatic mix of nature-lover and trendy fashionista, rushes our way.

"Tess? I've been buzzing your desk for the past half hour! What are you doing? You need to be manning the phone!"

"I'm on lunch break. Remember? I get one hour?"

"Well, not today." She nervously pulls her long blonde hair into a makeshift bun, a tribute to her California surfer-girl roots. "I need you at the front desk. I'm afraid this will leak to the press."

I stuff everything in my bag, standing. "What are

you talking about?"

"The bone." A sigh wracks her body, belying her well-disguised forty-plus years. "They found a *human* bone out back."

2

~*~

Bowhunting isn't something that comes naturally to everyone, and I understand your hesitation to develop this skill. Also, it is such a long trip to my special hunting grounds in wild and wonderful West Virginia. My great-grandpa is the one who owned the land I hunt, before the coal mine took it over. Now that mine is defunct. Riches are fleeting. I hope you learn that sooner rather than later. Your mother never will.

Hunting is an art, and a reprieve. I should feel guilty for traveling so far, for so many years, but I won't. I could either leave home for a season and regain some feeling of control or stay there and shrivel into a shell of a man. You don't deserve to see me that way. You deserve a father who can teach you how to control emotion by releasing an arrow, right into the heart of your prey.

This first trip will turn into a success, I just know

it. The best things in life come to those who wait.

Charlotte follows me inside. I charge straight through the halls, toward the pool entrance in back. To put a lid on this breaking news, I need to know what news has broken.

Three construction workers stand near their trucks, looking equal parts pale and enthused. I walk up to the one not wearing a hard hat, figuring he's the boss.

"What happened?"

He looks me up and down, and Charlotte jabs my arm with her elbow to let me know I'm being ogled. I point to him deliberately with my left hand, my wedding band and diamond catching the sunlight.

"I was talking to you. What's going on?"

His gaze sharpens, but he doesn't ask me who I am. Sometimes I can produce this authoritative effect. Thomas calls it my "commander vibe."

"It's like this, lady. We was digging this morning, right around sunrise. Me and my crew, we work hard, you know? And then Jack—that's him, right there with the overalls—he shouts that his shovel hit something hard. Course, we don't want to accidentally break no pipes, you understand."

I nod, knowing this guy is on a roll.

"So I said to stop and he stopped. Went over to check and lo and behold, there's this long thing in the dirt. Kinda deep...'bout five feet under. Ben got in there and pulled on it. Good thing he was wearing gloves because wouldn't you know, it was a bone! Weren't no dog bone neither. This was an arm bone, I'm pretty sure. Had some scraps of fabric on it, and the bone looked a little leathery."

"Where is it now?"

"Well, lady, we just dropped it back in the hole. Waiting on the cops or something now. Could even be the FBI! Sure does take them a while to get up to the top of this mountain."

I nod, stepping toward the hole. Sure enough, a long, brownish bone lies on top of the scooped-out pile of dirt. "Thanks for your help," I say, turning back to the spa.

Given what this guy has told me, I have good reason to man those phones. I imagine Tawny Creeden, the local hard news reporter—if there *is* such a thing in Buckneck—will be trekking her way up here as soon as word gets out.

Charlotte falls into step easily at my side as we wend through the dim-lit indoor pool area, past the nail room, and the sleek ebony-accented salon, where several hairdressers peer out windows, ignoring clients.

She talks in a hushed voice, like she's in a cathedral. "What do you think? Is that a human bone?"

"It's so long. It has to be...and I think I saw fingers."

Charlotte shudders. "How would that get there? Maybe this used to be a cemetery?"

I doubt it but don't want to assume the worst, as I'm wont to do. "No clue."

Back at the front desk, I settle into my chair, wishing for a strong cup of coffee. Charlotte grabs her purse. "I hate to go, but Mom's nurse needs to give me a report on things today. Will you drop by some night this week for cinnamon rolls and decaf?"

"Will do, if Thomas isn't working late." I hate asking my mother-in-law Nikki Jo to babysit, since she does during the days I work.

"Keep me posted. And I know you, Nancy Drew. Don't poke around too much."

"Who, me?"

During the next hour, I follow Dani's instructions and re-book appointments for next week. I speak softly into the phone, trying to console the ladies in their rescheduling pain.

Several times, Dani flits from her final henna job to my desk, her blue eyes asking the question she doesn't.

I fill her in each time. "No police yet." I'm astounded at the apparent lack of concern on the part of the Buckneck police. I contemplate calling Thomas at his law office, since he sometimes eats lunch with the local cops, but I realize that would only make Thomas drop everything and travel up here at breakneck speed. And if he knows, Nikki Jo would know. And if Nikki Jo knows about this bone...the whole town would know. Nothing against my mother-in-law, but that prayer chain is a powerful thing. Even if the poor person has been dead for fifty years, that bone would be cause for a prayer vigil. And I might get fired, which I really can't afford.

A man in camouflage strides through the double doors—definitely lost. He's almost past the desk when I stop him by rolling my chair over and flinging out an arm.

"Can I help you, sir?"

He turns. I'm struck by his dark eyes and thick salt-and-pepper hair and beard. "Yes, ma'am. You could." He pulls a badge from his pocket. "Detective Tucker. Buckneck P.D. I'm looking for Danielle...Gibson?"

As if on cue, Dani taps out to the reception desk. Her eyes are wide as she meets the detective's intense gaze. "I'm Danielle, the owner. Call me Dani." She extends a hand, and Detective Tucker takes it in both his own, like a father comforting a child. Like he's absorbing her nervousness.

"Show me the bone." A man of few words, wearing camo like a hunter in the middle of the day. I wonder if Thomas has met this character.

Dani walks him toward the back as the phone beeps again. I pick up quickly. "Crystal Mountain Spa, how may I help you?"

I recognize the wheedle in the voice before she gets to her name. "Hi. This is Tawny Creeden with *The Buckneck Daily*. I've heard that someone dug up bones on your property? Is this true?"

Tawny is known for having all the tact of a pig at the trough.

"I can't answer that. You'll have to talk with Dani, the owner. I can take your number—"

"No need. I'm on my way over now. I'll talk to her myself."

Our mutually snippy conversation concluded, I decide it's time to let Thomas know what's going on. Tawny knows at least two elderly women at church and she probably called them before she called me.

Thomas picks up on the first ring. "Tess. You okay?"

"Yes, hon—I don't know what you've heard—"

"Only that a human bone was found right behind where you work. I was hoping it was a hoax."

"Not really. I saw it myself."

"What! Did *you* find it? What's going on? I'm coming to get you."

"Calm down. I have the SUV here, remember? And it's just one bone. Granted, it does look like a human arm bone. But there is a detective here and everything is going to be fine—"

"A detective? Is he by any chance a mountain man who resembles a skinny George Clooney with a beard?"

"How did you know?"

"Detective Zechariah Tucker is not one to be trifled with. He's only pulled in for homicides. He spends most of his life hunting and camping in the woods, just like a real-live Bear Grylls. The only comfort I can take is that you'll be safe when he's around, because he repels bad guys. But could you please come on home? You know Mom will be in a state once she hears of this."

"Could you call her for me? I need to field the calls here and deal with a reporter for Dani. I promise I'll come home early tonight."

"You get out of there before dark or I will come and get you."

I hang up, thankful it's summer and it won't get dark till late. Although Thomas' sweet promise, similar to the "*I will find you*" line from *The Last of the Mohicans* movie, does touch me.

Detective Tucker thumps down the hallway with his combat boots. As he reaches my desk, he pulls a Coke bottle from his pocket and spits some tobacco juice into it, adding to the gritty black pool at the bottom. My eyebrows rise of their own accord and he notices.

"Dirty habit, I know. Not good for polite company, all that." He leans over the desk. "And you are...?"

"Tess Spencer, sir. My husband is a lawyer." I have no idea why I mentioned that.

"Thomas Spencer? Over with Meredith and Jenkins? I've seen him in court once or twice." He gives me a critical look, as if memorizing my hair and eye color, weight, and various other mug shot details. "A good man and a tough lawyer."

I immediately decide Detective Tucker and I will be fast friends. You like my husband, you like me.

"Mrs. Spencer. Were you out back when the bone was discovered?"

"No, sir. I was working. I had no clue what happened until our masseuse—Teeny—came and told us."

"Strange name."

"I agree."

We sit in companionable silence until the front door bursts open with a gust of wind. Tawny Creeden wrestles her briefcase, small video camera, and laptop in the door. Detective Tucker, his face impassive, walks straight past her, heading out to the parking lot. She doesn't pay him any attention, which shows me she has no idea who he is. Must not have covered a murder case before.

She dumps everything on one of the leather chairs, dislodging two pillows in the process. Thankfully, Dani chooses this moment to walk in and extends a hand.

"Danielle Gibson. I'm the spa owner. And you are?"

Tawny shakes hands, her long nails nearly poking Dani's wrist. "Tawny Creeden with *The Buckneck Daily*. We've heard some human bones were found on your property. I just have a few questions."

Dani smiles. I recognize that cat-that-ate-the-canary look. She has something up her sleeve.

"I'm sorry, Miss Creeden, but the detective on this case said no reporters. He has two policemen outside who are more than willing to remove anyone who interferes with the investigation."

"But that's not legal—" Tawny begins.

"Detective Tucker." Dani concludes.

Tawny scoops up her paraphernalia and huffs out the door.

"Well, that shut her down fast," I say.

"She knows who Detective Tucker is, even if she didn't recognize him. His reputation precedes him. Oh, well."

Dani's voice wavers and I take a second glance. All her bravado has evaporated. She drops into a chair. "I don't know how this happened. This is a homicide investigation now. I'm going to have to lay people off for a while. They found more bones."

3

~*~

I'm so glad we were able to hike and to go shooting on my colleague's land today. I underestimated your hunting skills. You have uncanny instincts, perhaps better than mine. You know which direction to go, picking up on the slightest sounds. You are a born predator.

And yet something is lacking. Some drive. You take after your mother in this way. She never had any goals in life other than to marry. I want more than that for you. Some of us are not meant for nuptials. I hope you realize this before it's too late and you are stuck, as I was. Amusing. The hunter became the prey. Your mother trapped me like a snared rabbit, with her beauty and charms. But I know something she doesn't. The universe always gives us a way out.

~*~

I continue fielding phone calls from customers and curious townspeople, barely looking up. Finally, my *Doctor Who* ringtone gives a whirring intergalactic shout-out, forcing me to yank my cell phone from the depths of my bag.

My husband doesn't waste time. "I'm outside."

I look out, and sure enough, dusk is falling fast. "Coming. Sorry, I just got busy. Let me find Dani and tell her I'm leaving."

I put the phone facedown and walk up the darkened hallway. The cloying smell of jasmine incense bubble-wraps any oxygen molecules I might hope to breathe. I play a hunch and veer toward the massage room. At my knock, Teeny opens the door on a candlelit scene, where Dani lies face down on the table.

She lifts her head, her face red from the cushion, blonde hair mussed. If I didn't know any better, I'd suspect some hanky-panky going on here. But the look in my boss' eyes shows she's far more freaked than romantic at this juncture.

"Tess? Good heavens. What time is it? Teeny offered a massage—my nerves are fried—and I lost track of everything. I just about passed out once or twice, I think."

Teeny gives a slight nod and warms more oil in his hands before working it into Dani's tan, toned back.

"I just wanted to let you know I'm heading home. What about tomorrow? I canceled all our appointments for this week, like you asked."

"You're a godsend. Honestly, I couldn't survive without you. Stay home tomorrow. Catch up with your baby girl. I'm not coming in to work and—" She tries to look up but winds up staring at the wall. "Teeny, you aren't either."

Teeny grunts his approval and applies extra pressure, propelling Dani's head back into the pillow. The conversation is closed. I want to ask about Detective Tucker and the next steps in the investigation, but Dani is one step away from catatonic and Thomas is waiting for me outside.

As I leave the overly warm room, I chill more than I should. Maybe I shouldn't leave Dani alone with Teeny. Is anyone else in the building? The lights are out everywhere else, so I'm assuming we're the last ones left.

A voice from the lobby steers me back—Thomas' voice blaring through the phone speaker. "You okay? Can you hear me?" I forgot I left him hanging there.

"Heading out now." I snatch the phone and my bags. Ever since I had a run-in with a demented killer last year, he's determined not to let me out of range.

Sure enough, Thomas waits for me just outside the

front door. As usual after work, he's yanked his tie loose instead of taking it off, which gives him that studied preppy look he's totally unaware of. He takes my bag and we follow the solar-lit footpath to the parking lot.

"So?" He wraps a long arm around me, pulling me close.

"Nothing much. I'm not going in to work the rest of the week."

"Well, that makes sense. You know, even though Dani looks like a washed-up surfer girl, she's remarkably astute."

"'Dani?' Since when do you know her on a first name basis?"

"Oh, we helped her set up the Crystal Mountain Spa a couple years ago. Didn't I tell you?"

Of course he didn't. When it comes to business, Thomas is admirably closed-lipped. I wonder if his clients realize the vault of silence my husband constructs around their secrets. He probably only told me this because it happened so long ago it has no bearing on anything.

"So...you met Detective Tucker. What did you think? Did he say anything about the case?" Thomas fumbles with the key to his old navy Volvo. No automatic door locks there.

"Nothing to me. I'm just an administrative assistant, remember?" I click my key-fob and my red

Escape lights up for me, beeping its enthusiasm. "You need a new vehicle, Thomas. That Volvo is on its last legs. I don't know how you can stand to drive around with no A/C in summer."

"We've talked about this before. There's no money for a new car. We'd need a serious windfall and for now, Freddie can keep it running."

Freddie is one of the oldest mechanics this side of Boone County and I'm beginning to think he's determined to give the Volvo as many years as he's had.

Thomas opens my SUV door with a flourish. "*Entrez vous*, m'lady." I climb in and he kisses my forehead. "We'll talk at home. Mom said she'll meet us at our cottage. She's already fed Mira Brooke."

A wave of joy catches me off-guard every time Thomas says our daughter's name. *Our* Mira Brooke, with the dark surprising curls and honey-soft skin. Our girl, who made me cry the first time she looked up and said *Mama*.

"See you there. You'd better go first in case your car gives up the ghost along the way."

"Very funny." He revs his engine and pulls out, and I throw a final glance at the spa. Is that a flashlight beam bouncing out back?

As we make our way down the Spencer family driveway, nearly every light is burning at Roger and Nikki Jo's big white house. I wonder if we should stop in at our in-laws', but Thomas rolls on by, to our cottage out back. The anemic bulb on our front porch lights a small circle, beckoning us in to the fully lit interior. Obviously Nikki Jo is a little worried.

She meets us at the door, handing Mira Brooke to me. I kiss my daughter's chubby cheeks while Mom talks.

"Ooh, honey. I heard. Everyone's wondering who on earth that is up there, dumped in the ground with no proper funeral or anything. Now it could be Widow-woman Charles. Goodness knows she's been missing some fifteen years. But most everyone believes she went and drowned herself in the Ohio River, even though they never did find her. Probably threw herself off the bridge."

Mira Brooke pats my face and then reaches for her daddy. Thomas takes her, absently kissing her head.

"Mom, do we really need to talk about this now? I'm tired; I'm sure Tess is tired..."

Nikki Jo places a manicured hand on her heart, obviously taken aback by Thomas' inability to play guess-who-died. I rush to her aid.

"It's hard to tell who it was. I figure they'll turn something up, though. It's Detective Tucker on the case."

"Zechariah? He went to school with me. Real quiet type, always noticing things. Shoot, he noticed my hair was permed before your daddy did, Thomas."

"Mm-hm." Thomas drops his tie and shirt on the couch, then hands Mira Brooke off to me. I know he's hungry, and sure enough, he heads right into the kitchen and fixes himself a plate of his mom's homemade ravioli and garlic bread.

"Well, whoever did this, I wouldn't want to go up against Zeke. He was an Eagle Scout and all that. Survivalist." Nikki Jo clacks her nails on the counter. "But Tess, you really shouldn't go back until they get all this straightened out. What if it's a recent killing?"

What if it's a recent killing? Nikki Jo, in typical candid fashion, just nailed what's been lurking in my thoughts all day, what I've been unwilling to consider. *What if* this isn't an old body? I don't know the rate of decomposition, but even a couple years back isn't very old for a murder.

"Don't worry, Mom. I'll be home a few days, at least, till this gets cleared up." Mira Brooke teases to get down, so I put her on the thick piece of carpet remnant Mom and Dad got us last year.

"Music to my ears." Nikki Jo swoops down to kiss her granddaughter, then hugs me and waves at Thomas. "See you tomorrow. Oh, and Petey said he'll stop by after school to gang shoot or something with you,

Tess."

I grin. Our "gang shoot" is in actuality a new Xbox multiplayer game we're working our way through. "Thanks, Mom."

As Nikki Jo closes the front door, Thomas saunters over, plate of ravioli carefully balanced in one hand. We watch in silence as Mira Brooke digs into her toy box, her dark cloud of curls bobbing.

He winks at me. "Hey shooter girl. You want to go real shooting with me sometime? Like for a date?"

Thomas is anxious for me to practice shooting, ever since I finally got my concealed carry permit. He bought me a smaller Glock, a nine millimeter, versus the .45 that kicked too much for me.

"Sure thing. I'll see when my schedule frees up." I grab his upper arm—solid muscle he somehow manages to maintain. Our playful banter quickly morphs into something charged, and he gives me a knowing look, dipping in for a kiss. Remarkably, his ravioli is still balanced in one hand.

"Hold your horses, lawyer man. I need to eat something."

"Oh, sure. Sorry. Me too. You're just distracting, wife."

His brown eyes simmer under ruffled blond bangs. My gaze travels again to his tan muscles extending beyond his T-shirt sleeves.

Mira Brooke squeals in delight, pushing a button

on a McDonald's Barbie toy that repeats some unintelligible phrase. Weakness washes over me and I dish up my food. One bite of Nikki Jo's cooking will boost my flagging spirits like restorative waters.

Thomas settles on the couch, prays silently, and begins to eat. "So...what was your impression of Detective Tucker?" He's fascinated with the mountain man detective.

"I don't know. Honestly, he didn't stand out. Chewing tobacco, camo—you know, your typical West Virginia guy. Thick hair for his age, I'd say—"

He interrupts, not interested in my descriptive prowess. "Some perps have turned themselves in, just knowing he was the primary investigator on their case." By the awe in his tone, I'd say Detective Tucker is one of the select few who impress Thomas.

Mira Brooke dances around with her toy, oblivious to how close she veers to the coffee table. I set my plate on the counter and rush toward her, but it's too late. She seems to fall in slow motion, cutting her head on the table's sharp edge.

My stomach lurches and I drop to her side. Blood, unnaturally red against her pale skin, trickles from a gash near her eyebrow, and she cries pitifully. Thomas hands me his napkin to stop the bleeding.

"What should I do?" he asks.

"Get the phone." I hold Mira Brooke close, pressing the napkin tight on the gash.

Thomas obediently retrieves my cell. "Should I call the emergency pediatrics number?"

"No, call your mom."

After Nikki Jo rushes over and pronounces it a surface cut, we find gauze and tape stanch the blood flow pretty quickly. I knew my mother-in-law would have a quick and accurate diagnosis, having raised three boys, two with serious daredevil propensities.

As I finally fall into bed, after bath duty and kitchen cleanup, it hits me. Mira Brooke's scheduled pediatrician appointment is tomorrow. And my worst nightmares will be realized: I'll look like a negligent mom, not so far removed from the one I grew up with.

4

~*~

Someone reported your mother to Social Services. I'll admit, it might have been me. I'm sick of seeing that woman's influence over you. She's making you soft.

In love, we have to make sacrifices. This is one of those times. I want you to remember everything I taught you. Tune out the lies your mother fed you and follow your own truth. I promise, I will find you someday and make sure you have followed the principles I have ingrained in you. I'll keep writing you letters, to make sure you understand I'm looking out for you.

Something might happen to your mother if she continues to press me. She is ungrateful and ignorant. I knew I had to free you to follow this text from the Atharva Veda: "Do not be led by others, awaken your own mind, amass your own experience, and decide for yourself your own path."

The pediatrician appointment leaves me steaming, but not because of an attack on my parental abilities. More like an attack on my personal liberties. When Dr. Lopez casually asked me if we had guns in the house, the answer was an immediate *yes*. After all, not only do I live in West Virginia, but I'm also married to a Spencer, and Spencer men have been proud gun owners from time immemorial. Mountaineers.

But I didn't ask for the stern lecture she gave me about guns, as if I had no idea how to handle them. And really, it was none of her business. I feel like there must be a law about this somewhere. I'll ask Thomas about it.

Mira Brooke, oblivious to my angst, kicks in her car seat and laughs. I have no clue where this child got her lighthearted spirit, but I hope she never loses it.

Suddenly, I realize I've turned the wrong way, as if my SUV has a mind of its own. We're heading toward The Haven, not toward home. But maybe this *is* the right way. I need to see the woman who has been my friend and surrogate grandma for so many years, even if she doesn't recognize me.

I give Mira Brooke a couple animal crackers and head to the front desk. A smarmy new receptionist greets me, asking twenty questions before finally allowing us down the hall to Miranda's room.

Technically, Miranda Michaels should not be in this assisted living home, especially in her current condition. But Miranda's money opens doors that would be shut to ordinary people. And yet one of the reasons everyone loves her is that she never lets on how wealthy she is. Yes, she has expensive jewelry and nice furniture. But she has always made me feel beautiful in my consignment-store jeans and Payless shoes.

I tap at her door and a hushed nurse opens it. "I'm here to see Miranda," I whisper.

Mira Brooke's cracker hits the floor, and a wail splits the air. Maybe this wasn't the best idea.

Charlotte rushes from the bedroom, nearly knocking the nurse over. "I recognize that cry!" Taking Mira Brooke from my arms, she snuggles into her downy hair. Tears glisten in her eyes.

The nurse sidles into the hallway. "I need to check on a couple patients."

As she shuts the door, Charlotte sighs. "God knew I needed to see this baby girl. Mom's pulse has been all over the place and this new nurse makes it sound like she's going to go at any moment."

I put my hand on Charlotte's arm. "I'm so sorry. I'll have a talk with the nurse."

Charlotte shakes her head. "Some people just don't

have a great bedside manner, that's all." She sniffs and smiles. "I don't think Mom's ready to go yet. Anyway, go on in and see her. She's...well, you know. I tell you what, I'll get this little sweet pea a snack." Without another word, she whisks Mira Brooke into the tiny kitchen.

My breath catches as I step into the familiar bedroom. The pleasant smell of body lotion wafts my way, and I follow it to the tiny, pale woman lying under a maroon velour bedspread.

I take her shriveled hand in mine, finally bringing myself to look in her eyes. It's amazing how much someone can change in a year. In Miranda, the loss of strength is heartbreaking. Her once-sharp eyes trail over my features, with no spark of recognition.

"Miranda." I clear my throat and try again. "Miranda, it's me, Tess. You know, that young'un you used to stomp at chess."

I squeeze her hand tighter, wishing for her familiar laugh to fill the spaces in my awkwardness. Her snow-white head tips forward and her eyes drop slightly.

"Well...I'll tell you what. I have a job now, can you believe it? And you know I named my baby girl after you. I'd bring her in, but she's wiggly as all get-out right now. Charlotte might as well be her aunt, she fawns on her so much. You remember she's staying in your big green house? It's so nice to have her close. We sure did make friends, just like you wanted."

Miranda looks like she's falling asleep. I'm not telling her anything new, but I had hoped for some sign of recognition. I try to channel some of my hand's warmth into the coldness of her palm.

"Anyway, there's been some news...not to shock you, but then again, I know you're not easily shocked. They found some bones up at the Crystal Mountain Spa where I work—it's up on Grover's Mountain. Do you know a man named Zechariah Tucker? He's the head detective."

I sigh, knowing there will be no response. Mira Brooke's laughter drifts in from the living room and I realize why I really came: to admit my shortcomings as a mother. To be absolved.

"My Mira Brooke hit her head last night. Turned into a big bruise for her doctor appointment today."

Miranda's head slowly rises, her watery blue eyes focusing on me. I can hear her voice funneling into my head, even though she doesn't say a word. "*Every child gets hurt, and goodness knows mothers can't protect them from everything. But Tess Spencer, you'd lay down your life for that child. She'll grow up just fine.*"

Charlotte knocks lightly on the door. "The nurse is back to check on her. Sorry."

I pull my hand slowly from Miranda's. Somehow we're still connected. She always knows how to speak to what weighs heaviest on my heart, even if she can't speak at all.

"Sure, of course." I smile. "Thanks, Miranda."

Charlotte gives me a questioning look, but like her momma, she understands when I don't want to talk about something. She passes a contented Mira Brooke off to me. As we walk to the suite door, she asks, "So, any word on that weird bone?"

I give a short whistle. "I forgot to let you know— they found more bones."

"What? Maybe it was just some old hick graveyard they turned up, then. No headstones, they just buried them deep—"

"Don't think so. There's a police detective on the case now. I can't even go into work until next week. I'll keep you posted as I learn things."

"You'd better! I wish you hadn't taken that job at the spa in the first place. Dani, with all her New-Age mumbo-jumbo...Teeny, with his nonstop come-ons and oversized body..."

"You worry too much about me."

Charlotte offers her familiar refrain. "Someone has to!"

In the hallway, I nearly bump into a man who looks like he works there. "So sorry."

The sandy-haired man mutters something, then shuffles closer, jabbing a finger toward my face. I hold Mira Brooke tighter, pressing her cheek into my chest.

An aide rushes up. "Mr. Seger. It's nearly gardening time." She whispers my way, "I'm sorry, ma'am. He's new here and he's easily excited."

I nod, moving away from the fractious man. One good thing about Miranda's condition is that she won't be exposed to someone like him. He really seems on the young side for an assisted living home, but you never can tell.

Back in the SUV, my cell phone jams with the *Buffy the Vampire Slayer* ringtone. I wanted to set Dani's calls apart and since Buffy is blonde, I somehow connected the two.

She cuts her usual pleasantries. "I have a problem."

"What's going on?"

"I know I said you could have the next few days off, but the IT guy is coming to fix our computer system. It crashed last night. I already have an appointment tomorrow, and you're the only other one who knows the computers. Could you by any chance be there from nine to three-ish? I'll pay you double."

Extra pay for minimal work is always nice. "Sure, no problem. I assume the police will be there too?"

"Yes, but they can let themselves in and out. I gave Detective Tucker a key, although I figure that man could get in without one if he needed to."

"Right. Okay, I'll be there."

As I pull from my parking space, the bothersome Mr. Seger bursts from The Haven's front doors and rushes toward me, his aide lagging a bit behind.

I hit the brakes as he runs in front of my car, then crack my window to shout. "Watch out!"

Mr. Seger saunters over. "*Excusez-moi*, madam. I was just on my way to a concert, you understand. Running a bit behind schedule."

The harried aide grabs his elbow. "Can't keep this one in the building. He escaped yesterday too." As she nudges him back toward The Haven, she twirls her finger near her forehead.

Thomas is right. I have a habit of attracting crazies. And something tells me there's no easy way to fix that.

5

~*~

So sorry to hear you're in foster care. I hope you find a good home. I'll be away a while. You understand I have things to take care of.

Of course I expect you took your bow and arrows with you. If they didn't let you, write me at the post office box number on the envelope and I will be sure to deliver some. It is imperative you continue practicing your marksmanship. I can only hope you don't end up in some suburban house with a postage-stamp yard. Still, there are shooting ranges, I imagine, or woods nearby where you could practice.

Good bowhunters can be made, but excellent bowhunters like us are born.

I'm trying to avoid contact with your mother. It's just safer that way. I'm looking at this as a healthy separation for us. You will only grow stronger under the pressures of the system. I'll come and find you when you turn sixteen, then we can hunt together in earnest. I'll keep writing so you don't forget me.

In the morning, I find Mom cleaning house like a fiend. Andrew, her middle son, is coming home from college this week and Nikki Jo never knows when he'll have a girlfriend in tow. I settle Mira Brooke in with Dad in the TV room, dropping off her snacks in the kitchen where Nikki Jo will see them. Although I'm sure Nikki Jo has something far tastier than Cheerios and applesauce planned for my girl's lunch.

By the time I get to the spa, several police vehicles sit in the parking lot. There's also one camouflage Hummer that resembles a tank. I suspect this belongs to the illustrious Detective Tucker.

Sure enough, he's lounging at the door, this time sporting saddle-colored Carhartt overalls. It strikes me again just how unobtrusive this man is. He could be anybody off the street; you'd never notice him. The only way he stands out is when he gives you that deep measuring look. If I were a criminal on the receiving end of that look, I'd rightly panic and flee.

Instead, his gaze shifts from me to the white minivan pulling into the lot. "Who's that?"

I squint to read the small print on the side, an

ineffective marketing job if ever I've seen one. "D&R Computer Tech. That's the IT guy. He's supposed to be here."

"Keep him in the main room, please, Mrs. Spencer. We can't have him wandering back to the dig."

He says "dig" like it's an archeological adventure. If only they *were* turning up something amazing, like a T-Rex, instead of dead bodies.

"Will do." I feel entrusted with a sacred mission.

Detective Tucker wanders off toward the building and I greet the repair guy, who's tugging a heavy-looking leather satchel from his side door.

"Hi, I'm Tess. I'll show you inside."

The IT man looks up at me, and our eyes meet. His black horn-rimmed glasses hide bright blue eyes, and his geek-chic plaid shirt fits him perfectly. This guy looks like a thirty-something model masquerading as a computer repairman. A bright and somewhat dazzling smile spreads across his face. "No problem. Lead the way."

As I walk up the path, he continues talking. "My name is Byron Woods. Byron as in Lord Byron. My mom was into poets."

I wouldn't mind getting into a conversation about poets, but I want to streamline this thing so I can get out of here earlier. I show him to the main desk and log into the computer. As I grab myself another chair, he settles down and starts tapping away.

Since I have no clue what happened to the computers last night, I just let him poke around. The spa feels dead with no Enya piping overhead and no candles flickering. Usually Dani comes in early and lights about twenty candles in the reception area. I always worry someday it'll burn the place down—this is a giant log cabin, after all—but it's her spa to do with as she likes.

After thirty minutes listening to nothing but the sound of clicking keys, restlessness drives me from my seat to the snack room. I plunder the fridge for anything edible to tide me over. Dani regularly brings homemade food to share, but usually it's things like wheatgrass pancakes or unsweetened fruit bars. I prefer a little sugar with my life.

I finally turn up a container of frozen spring rolls that somehow made the healthy cut and pop them in the microwave. While they're heating, I peek into the darkened hallway, then tiptoe toward the indoor pool. The floor-to-ceiling glass windows give an unobstructed view of the digging machinations outside.

They haven't wasted time. The earth is stripped away from a gaping hole, marked off by the inevitable crime scene tape. I look beyond the police photographer to the bones, shuddering at the skull staring right up at me. Hard to grasp there might be entire skeletons lying down there.

A voice murmurs near my ear, making me jump. "What's that?"

Byron, the inquisitive IT man, has flown the coop. I have to get him out of the pool room before he sees anything.

He peers out the window, pushing his glasses up his nose as if to process things better. "Wait. Are those...bones?"

I grab his arm, but the minute my fingers inadvertently wrap around a well-honed muscle, I drop my hand. Instead, I gesture wildly to the front desk.

"How are the computers? Were you able to fix the problem? What was wrong? Was it a virus?" If we're playing Twenty Questions, I can win.

"What? Oh, yes. I found the problem. But it's not a virus. I'll show you."

I turn our conversation to poetry as we walk back to the desk. Turns out Byron isn't excessively fond of Lord Byron, but prefers Robert Frost. I explain my college fascination with Sylvia Plath and my subsequent disillusionment with everything she wrote once I got married, which is when life started to make sense.

At the front desk, Byron elaborates for twenty minutes on things I could never possibly understand. I stifle a yawn but perk up when a weathered woman in head-to-toe black leather motorcycle garb waltzes through the door.

"Can I help you?" My Southern manners fly out the window. Normally I say *May I help you, ma'am?* It's been a funky day at the Crystal Mountain Spa, and this woman doesn't resemble our normal clientele.

She grips her helmet, extending her hand to me, which is encased in a tough-looking fingerless glove. "I sure hope so. I made a wrong turn earlier but kept going because I enjoyed the view. Then I realized I'm nearly out of gas. What's the chance there's a gas station somewhere around?"

Byron interjects an unexpected comment. "There actually is one. If you follow that trail that runs through the woods, it'll come out near a truck stop." He peers out the front window. "Your bike should be able to handle it. Someone keeps it cleared off."

She takes a long, appreciative look at him, then glances back at me for confirmation. How did Byron know this tidbit about a path through the woods?

I shrug. "I had no idea, but there is a cleared area back in there." Shifting gears, I ask, "So, what brings you to these parts? You don't sound local."

She sighs. Static tugs at the outer strands of her long dark hair, sending it flying. "I'm taking some time off from my marriage...seeing the country. Carpe Diem, you know. I've never been this far east." She puts her helmet on. "I'd better run so I can find a place to eat and stay overnight. Much obliged."

After a slow wink at Byron and a grin at me, she

strides out the door, black fringes fluttering on her jacket. The motorcycle revs and bumps around the porch onto the grass.

Byron pauses, then launches back into the description of the computer problem. He finally sums it up by declaring he'll need to return the next few days as well. For now, he needs to go since he, too, forgot to bring lunch.

A good ten minutes after Byron leaves, Detective Tucker stamps dirt off his feet and pushes through the front doors. I suspect he was keeping an eye on Byron.

He spits into his bottle. "What're your thoughts on that one?"

Under his scrutiny, I cave and admit my sad lapse in guard duties. "He kind of snuck up behind me and saw the bones—sorry. He asked a couple questions but I diverted him." I glance up at him casually. "By the way, how many bodies are out there?"

The detective's lips quirk upward at my question. "Most women wouldn't stand around looking at skeletons, but evidently you're not like most women."

I smile too, understanding he's evading my question.

"To be honest, Mrs. Spencer, we're not quite sure yet. Still piecing things together."

I'm not sure if he meant to make a pun, because he doesn't smile. Boldness floods me. "Were they murdered?"

His dark gaze gets nearly black. "Between you, me, and this desk, yes. I'll report on things to your boss soon enough. But if you're going to be coming and going, I'd recommend you be careful."

I thought law enforcement was supposed to encourage people to be calm, not worry, and things like that. Instead, Detective Tucker is telling me to watch my back.

"Will do." I stifle the urge to ask why.

Another black stream shoots from his mouth and into the bottle. Horrible habit, chewing.

He seems to pick up on my attitude and saunters toward the back. But before he's out of sight, he says, "Mrs. Spencer, do you conceal carry?"

"Why would you ask that? It's not illegal."

"No. I was actually going to recommend you should. So far, all those bodies are women."

6

~*~

This first year of your absence has hit me hard, but then I remind myself you are growing into who you need to be, just as I am growing in the space apart from your mother. She's written me exactly three times and called me once, begging me to come back. The woman doesn't know what's good for her. I hate how she spouts poetry like some lovesick fool. Certainly, quote Rumi, quote Confucius, but don't go quoting rhymey nonsense like Donne and tell me it has any pith to it.

What your mother doesn't understand is that when mistakes are made, we can let them define us or we can use them to our advantage. Our marriage was a mistake, but of course you were not. Your mother and I just aren't capable of rearing you as a proper unit.

Some days I will admit I miss you badly, but I remind myself this isn't the only life we have. What isn't done right the first time around can be rectified in our following lives.

By the time we are reunited in a few years, we will be stronger than ever. Are you target shooting?

I call Dani before I head out at two, hoping she can fill in for me tomorrow with computer duties. Instead, she begs off.

"So sorry, Tess. I have some family stuff going on. I would've had to miss work one way or another. Was it horribly dreadful?"

I decide not to give her any gruesome details. "Detective Tucker will talk to you soon," I hedge.

As I wind down the mountain, I wonder about the motorcyclist. Did she make it okay to the truck stop? I can't imagine undertaking a cross-country motorcycle jaunt on my own. I wonder if *she* has a concealed carry permit. That would get tricky because each state has different laws.

The town of Buckneck has its patriotic game face on, thoroughly bedecked for the Fourth of July. Baskets of red geraniums hang from the wrought-iron streetlamps. Most houses are festooned with some sort of starred and striped decorations, and one well-shorn lawn has red, white, and blue stars spray-painted on it.

Original.

I grit my teeth as I pass the familiar brown-and-orange Meredith and Jenkins, LLP sign. The name Spencer *should* be on there—in very fact, it should be front and center. My husband does more work than Royston Jenkins, and Jack Meredith happens to be dead. But years into this gig, Royston still hasn't asked Thomas to become partner.

I'm tempted to drop in on Charlotte and give her the day's scoop, but she's probably at The Haven anyway. Besides, I need down-time with Mira Brooke. I took this job because I could have part-time hours, but this week it feels like I've practically moved in at the spa.

Petey opens the door at the big house for me. I ruffle his mop of red hair. "You're getting taller every day, cute little punk."

He grins, showing the bright green bands on his new braces. "You know it. Someday I'll be the tallest Spencer of all."

The family dog, a miniature Pinscher named Thor, clicks up to me, then sits and wags his tail. I stare. "Is it my imagination, or is this dog learning some manners?"

"I've been reading up on obedience training since Ma said she absolutely won't spring for it. I figured out I might be a dog whisperer."

"Either that, or Velvet and Thor had some smackdown cage fight we missed."

We laugh. My white fluff-ball cat, Velvet, has more than enough attitude to take on dogs three times her size. Most of the time she's inside, but sometimes she escapes and tries to give Thor a what-for.

"How's Mira Brooke?"

"Come on in and see for yourself. Dad's kept an eye on her all day, but Ma lit into him when he let her take a nap on his chest. Said she could fall outta the chair or something."

I follow Petey into the kitchen, where Mira Brooke sits in her baby seat, stuffing banana slices into her mouth. When she sees me, she squeals and throws her arms out, scattering sticky pieces everywhere.

I plant a big smooch on her forehead and Nikki Jo comes over with a wet paper towel to clean up the mess. "The house looks great," I say. "You planning a big Fourth blowout while Andrew's in?"

She sighs. "Blamed if I knew what his plans are. He said something about a little surprise. I'd like to know what gave him the notion I enjoy surprises. But yes—I want us to celebrate, no matter what he's up to this trip."

We stand in silence a moment, remembering that awkward Christmas with Helga, the Icelandic girlfriend who spoke halting English. It's entirely possible things will get worse before they get better on Andrew's dating front.

Petey perks up. "Tess, you have time to play a couple rounds?"

Much as I love playing video games with my brother-in-law, I need to spend more of my limited time with my daughter. "How about this weekend when I'm off work, okay?"

Petey gives an exaggerated sigh, then trudges off toward his room.

Nikki Jo springs right into her questioning as I extract Mira Brooke from the chair. "So...did they find anything? Was Zeke there?"

Erring on the side of too little information, I tell Nikki Jo they're still digging and aren't sure how many bodies there are, which is entirely true.

"I have to go back tomorrow, though. Stinking computer stuff."

"Sorry, Tess. Well, I'll be around and Andrew will be getting here, too. Roger has to go to his Veterans' Club meeting. Just you rest your mind about Mira Brooke." She squeezes her granddaughter's cheeks. "She's the light of my life, aren't you, sugar cube?"

Mira Brooke lunges for her grandma. I wonder if she'll ever know my mom or feel the same warmth toward her. Probably not, since my mom is in the Alderson Women's Prison and hasn't called me since last year. I have a feeling drug rehab isn't going as well as they'd hoped.

~ ✳ ~

I settle a squeaky-clean Mira Brooke in my lap, reveling in her soft Johnson's Baby Shampoo smell. She snuggles into me, her chubby legs and arms swathed in fluffy pink pajamas. Her fair little fingers grip my hand as I begin to read a story from one of her thick board books.

I've nearly nodded off like Mira Brooke when my phone rings with Charlotte's distinctive *Wonder Woman* ringtone. I pick up.

"You there?"

"Yes. What's going on?"

She sounds like she's walking, feet crunching gravel. "Nothing. But I'm here—outside your house. Can I visit a little?"

"Sure. Hang on while I put Mira Brooke in her crib."

I tiptoe upstairs, checking to make sure the baby monitor is on before shifting Mira Brooke into Petey's old crib. Thank goodness she's a sound sleeper, like her dad. She barely stirs.

Outside the front door, Charlotte furiously bats at moths with her jade green envelope clutch. She's one of the few people on earth who could look elegant doing this.

I hug her, catching a whiff of her rose-citrus

perfume. I'm not sure what I smell like this time of day, but it sure isn't rose-citrus.

"Coffee? I have some apple pie Nikki Jo sent over yesterday."

Charlotte nods and makes a beeline for the couch, dropping into it. If we didn't get along so well, her quietness would be unnerving. While I'm scooping fresh grounds into my French press, Charlotte finally pipes up.

"I'm dating."

I peer around the partition that separates the kitchen and living room, trying to hide my surprise. "Well...that's good!"

She frowns. "You think so? At a time like this?"

"*Especially* at a time like this. You need someone to lean on, someone to be there when your mother can't. I know these past months have been grueling on you, Charlotte."

"Right. I mean, it's already July. The university has contacted me about teaching Ceramics next semester. They want to make me an Associate Professor. I'm starting to think I should go back, just to get my mind off everything."

I serve up the pie on small plates, thoughts whirring. West Virginia University is all the way over in Morgantown, a good two and a half hours away. If Miranda gets worse or if anything happens, I'll be first in line to deal with it. Which I don't mind, but what if I do something wrong? I can't bear for our friendship to be severed.

Charlotte walks into the kitchen to help. "I see that look on your face. Don't stress it. I'll check in with The Haven every day. Mom has a private nurse, remember? I can get back here fast if something happens."

We sip our coffee in silence. Finally, the curiosity overtakes me. "So...who are you dating?"

She laughs—a rich sound I will miss so much. "You're not going to believe this."

"Hit me."

Stretching her long fingers, as if she's gearing up to sculpt some pottery, she gives me a sheepish look. "The Good Doctor."

I suck in my breath. "But his daughter is your age!"

"See, I knew you wouldn't like it."

Doctor Bartholomew Cole, whom we'd nicknamed The Good Doctor, was a major person of interest when I was hunting down Rose Campbell's killer last year. Even though he was exonerated, it's still awkward when I run into him doing rounds at The Haven.

Charlotte shovels a bite of pie in her mouth. "Please don't lecture me. Of course I know how old he is. I told you I *like* older men."

The steel edging Charlotte's words warns me to back off. Anyway, I want to be happy for my lonely friend.

"But if you leave?"

"I'll be here this summer. Doc—*Bartholomew*—can keep me posted on Mom when I go."

"But Rosemary?"

The Good Doctor only discovered Rosemary was his daughter last year and I wonder if he's had any success getting to know her. The woman has been hostile to us on more than one occasion.

"She's...well, she's Rosemary, you know? Driving around in that big truck, smoking like a chimney. I need to spend more time with her, but it's hard with my mom."

"No, don't waste time trying to get on her good side. I figure if she's going to like you, she will. So does she at least get along with her dad?"

"They've met up a few times. She's back at work at the Bistro Americain. I hear she makes a regular salary in tips alone."

We laugh. It's not a stretch to believe the curvy, flirty Rosemary would be well tipped.

Seriousness darkens her eyes. "Really, Tess, I'm more concerned about leaving you. What about this bone dig? Is this a dangerous situation? Does Thomas know there are more bodies?"

It's a gentle rebuke. Charlotte knows I haven't told Thomas. It's not that I want to hide things from him, but sometimes he just can't handle the truth. After all, I'm doing my job, raking in some income for our little family. I can't help it if there are dead women's bodies turning up at my workplace.

"Perfectly safe. The place is crawling with cops. Zechariah Tucker is allegedly the bane of criminal masterminds everywhere, and he's the lead detective. So I'm not worried."

"No, you're not," Charlotte says slowly. "And that's what worries me."

7

I've met with a psychologist twice, at the dean's insistence. He said I needed a break from teaching, so I've been put on hold, as it were, for a year. I explained to him that life is suffering and our separation is just a natural part of things. Before I can understand anyone, I must understand myself. I need this time for introspection, for renewal.

I had a letter from your foster mother, Karen. I can't imagine how she got my address, but perhaps you shared it with her? I'd rather you tell no one where I am now. I don't want your mother harassing me again. Karen said you are the model child, making straight A's. She urged me to bring you home, but of course she doesn't understand our situation. I am not ready to support you and I am a bit distressed that she would even suggest it. What does she look like, this caregiver of yours? Is she single? Kind? Perhaps I should look in on her.

Or perhaps I should visit you; take you on a trip. I have not visited West Virginia in a long while.

"Wish I didn't have to work these long hours." Thomas nuzzles me with his morning-stubbled face. "This neglect case requires so much time. These things are so draining but no one else will touch them."

I know that's about all he'll tell me, but it's obvious his work weighs heavy on his mind. It strikes me that I could've been a neglect case. I learned to fix my meals at a fairly young age because my mom was either working or too tired to come up with something. I ran around wherever I wanted in the trailer park, even at night. My afterschool program consisted of memorizing snippets of my neighbors' conversations as the words drifted from their windows. And yet, by the grace of God, I survived, and now I'm able to thrive in the Spencer family.

I smooch Thomas' cheek, then his lips. Unruly blond bangs drop over his eye and I smooth them back. "I love you," I whisper. Tears flood my eyes.

He understands I'm thinking about my mom. "It's been a while, hasn't it? Wonder if there's some reason she can't write or call."

"I don't know. I wrote her after the shootout at Rose's. You'd think she could call or write to say she's glad I survived."

He nods. "So what's going on at the spa? Mom said you have to go in today? I thought Detective Tucker was still there."

I roll out of bed and stretch. "He is. They're still investigating. But Dani needed me to be around for the computer repair guy."

Thomas raises his eyebrows.

"Don't freak. I'm going to take the Glock."

He nods in approval. "As long as Detective Tucker is around, I won't worry."

Much as I like Detective Tucker, I will worry until my Glock is securely tucked in its holster. Its familiar weight on my belt is a tangible reminder of the weight of responsibility I carry with it.

"There's something we need to talk about sometime." Thomas strips off his shirt, prepping for the shower. I try to read his glance: perturbed? stressed? excited? Those hazelnut-brown eyes tell me nothing.

"Okay, sure. How about supper tonight? Maybe I could make meatball subs."

Thomas strides to the bathroom. "Thanks, but how about I treat you? We can have a home-date. I'll pick up subs from Giorelli's. Maybe Mom wouldn't mind babysitting Mira Brooke a little later tonight, especially since Andrew's coming in. He'll want to see her, too."

I throw my arms around him. "You're an angel to me, and worth your weight in gold. We'll talk tonight."

I pull into the spa parking lot, next to Byron's van. He's nowhere in sight, but I can't see far in this early-morning fog. Here on top of Grover's mountain, you're often sitting smack in the middle of a cloud.

As I unhook my seatbelt, I touch the frame of my Glock, reminding myself I don't have to be afraid. Last year's showdown with a revolver-wielding psychopath taught me one unforgettable lesson: don't take a knife to a gun fight.

Fog snatches my voice and muffles it as I call out in the parking lot. "Byron? Anybody here?"

Someone jogs my way. Byron's dark hair and glasses come into view, emerging from the mist like some bodiless alien. "Hey there, Tess. I was just waiting for you up at the spa."

Only he wasn't waiting at the front door, like a normal person would. He came from around back, where the bodies were.

"See any police?" I ask.

He looks surprised. "No. Why, are they still around?"

So he's going to play dumb. "Sure are, and they're

not going to appreciate you sneaking around their dig. Come on inside."

As I unlock the door, I can almost feel Byron's glare, burning holes in the back of my head. I don't need to apologize for warning him to stay where he's supposed to.

Teeny meets us at the door, shifting from one foot to the other like he has to go to the bathroom. He gives Byron a once-over, then ignores him. "Tess, I have a couple massages today. Could you just send them on back when they get here?"

"But there's nothing on the books." I boot up the computer, then move out of Byron's way as he sets up his laptop.

"These are on my own time." Teeny offers no other explanation.

While I'm pretty sure my administrative duties don't extend to taking Teeny's personal appointments, I'll make an exception since I have nothing else vying for my time. "Sure thing. By the way, have you seen any cops here today?"

Teeny laughs—a heavy, braying sound. "Nope. Must be sleeping in." He shambles on down the hall.

I can't imagine Detective Tucker abandoning a hotspot littered with skeletons. Something else must have come up...something big.

~*~

Byron taps at keys, chews on pens, and generally drives me nuts for hours with his nervous energy. When an overly-tanned platinum blonde shows up, I steer her toward the massage room. I wonder what kind of gig Teeny is running. I'll be sure to mention this next time I talk to Dani, although I wonder what she's up to anyway. What kind of owner abandons her business when dead bodies show up?

Around eleven, a police car pulls in. Detective Tucker makes for our front door while his underlings go around back. Today he's wearing faded Wranglers and a beat-up Dr. Pepper T-shirt. Topping the look is a WVU baseball cap, which lends an oddly distinguished air to the ensemble.

Byron glances up but doesn't say a word. Detective Tucker motions for me to follow him down the hall. He stalks into the hair salon, closes the door behind me, and plops down in a styling chair.

"Something's come up."

"What?"

"Woman went missing yesterday. She was seen going into a truck stop bathroom, but no one saw her leave. Reason I'm telling you is that it's not far from here."

A heaviness drops on me, literally pushing me to a

sitting position in the closest chair. Sudden nausea rises. I rest my head in my hands.

"You okay?" He walks to my side.

I can't really say I am, but I push past my light-headedness. "The woman...did she have a motorcycle?"

"Sure did. It was left there overnight, which is why the employees started to wonder. How'd you know?"

"We saw her yesterday. She came by the spa, looking for a gas station. Byron—the computer repair guy—he told her how to take a shortcut through the woods to get there."

"Oh, right, I remember hearing that engine rev. Did she give you any information as to who she was, where she was from?"

I replay her words in my mind: "*I'm taking some time off from my marriage...seeing the country. Carpe Diem, you know. I've never been this far east.*" I repeat them to Detective Tucker. "She didn't say her name. Do you think something happened to her? She was looking for a place to eat and stay overnight."

"Could've been any number of things, since no one saw her leave and the surveillance cameras don't cover that area. She could have taken a ride from someone or walked to a restaurant. Her gas tank wasn't filled. We've searched the truck stop and asked at local hotels and hospitals, but so far, nothing." He gives me a searching look. "You feeling any better? You looked like you were going to pass out."

I nod, slowly straightening up. Probably nothing happened to her. But I admire that woman...her *joie de vivre*, her excitement to be on an adventure. What kind of bravery does it take to travel cross-country on a motorcycle? I hope things will work out with her husband, if he's a good man.

An ashen-faced cop stumbles into the salon, absently brushing dirt from his pants onto the clean white tiles. He looks at me and hesitates, but Detective Tucker nods. "Go on. News?"

The young policeman sucks in one long breath, then speaks. "We found her, sir. She's out back, buried in a shallow hole right near the others. Sir, she has an arrow through her chest."

8

~*~

This time I gave that vapid psychologist something to write about. I told her what I've been thinking about your mother, that she needs to be eradicated like a putrid infection. I daresay I raised her eyebrows a couple times as I described how that woman piques me.

The more I mull over it, the more I realize how your mother's personality was all wrong for me. Churchgoing, needy, always taking my income and refusing to work and make her own. Honestly, how would any man not get exhausted with demands like that, in the face of all that righteous stubbornness? The only way to escape her is to visit my woods and hunt, like I did as a teen, when my own mother tried to control everything I did. What miniature tyrants mothers are!

Of course, I feel I've invested enough time in you that you won't hold to your mother's beliefs. You'll see how fickle her God is, this God who says he's the only one in the universe. Impossible. As you know, I'm well-versed on religions and they're all the same, infused with moral codes we naturally obey. To end suffering, we must rid the world of greed and ignorance. Your mother can't see this, because greed and ignorance drive her to go against me. I can't seem to educate her so I had to remove myself from her, to minimize my suffering.

I got your letter and I do hope things are going more smoothly in this new foster home. It's really too bad you have to be moved around so much. Just keep sharing good energy and things will work out in your favor.

Somehow I muddle through a couple more hours in the waiting room with Byron, who's taken to muttering to himself before each fresh burst of typing. I keep picturing his ghostly face, emerging from the fog. He knew the motorcyclist was heading to the truck stop yesterday. He left soon after she did. But what would possess Byron to stalk and kill an older married woman? There seems no clear motive.

And Teeny. He was here early too. While it's easy to picture Teeny snapping someone's neck or punching them in the carotid, it's also entirely possible that he's handy with a bow. He could have buried her body before I arrived at the spa.

I wonder about that arrow. Maybe she didn't even die from being shot with it. Maybe the killer shoved it in after strangling her or clonking her on the head with a rock.

But if it was murder by arrow, that necessitates premeditation to the utmost degree. Someone could be lurking outside the spa even now, watching each cop leave, waiting for an opportunity to kill another woman. Even my Glock won't save me from a killer I can't see.

Byron touches my arm lightly, almost sensually. I cross my arms and stand. "You finished?"

"Probably one more day will do it. You mind letting me in tomorrow?" He blinks rapidly, like he's gearing up for me to cross-question him on it.

I probably should. I may not know much about computers, but taking three days to fix one must be overkill. Still, I don't want to waste time with another of his obtuse explanations. I have a feeling D&R Computer Tech is taking Dani for all she's worth. In the end, it might have been cheaper to replace the computers.

"I'll check with Dani and she'll let you know."

He opens his mouth, doubtless preparing to tell me why it's crucial he returns, but Detective Tucker strides in. Even in casual clothes, he exudes a certain menace. Maybe it's the Julius Caesar haircut, or the zealous look he gets when questioning people. I find myself hoping I'll never disappoint him. He's like a tamed wolf. If he loves you, you're gold. If he turns on you, you're dead.

Sweat glistens on Byron's forehead, the only sign he's nervous as he shakes Detective Tucker's hand. "Byron Woods."

"Detective Tucker. You still hanging around here?"

"Yes, I'm just fixing the computers. Should be finished tomorrow."

Detective Tucker pulls out his ever-present Coke bottle and spits into it. He doesn't say one word, just stares at Byron.

Byron shifts on his neatly loafered feet, shooting me a hopeful glance. I don't interject a comment. If he killed that motorcyclist, he should squirm.

"You talk to that drifter woman yesterday? Mrs. Spencer here tells me you gave her directions to that truck stop."

"She was asking where to get gas. It's the only place nearby, and I knew her bike could handle that path. I used to bike a little myself."

"You don't say." Another tobacco stream hits the fast-blackening bottle. "Be here tomorrow, buckaroo."

Byron flinches at the word *buckaroo*, but rallies fast. "Yes, I'll see you then...thanks." He heads to the door.

Detective Tucker makes a shooing motion with his hand, as if sweeping Byron out faster. When Byron reaches his van, the detective finally speaks.

"This is a bad business. Broadhead arrow through the chest, just like the others—the bodies we've exhumed were killed the same way. Only difference is the killer removed those arrows after death. Which means the wacko watched those women bleed out. Given where he hit them—heart and lungs—it probably happened fast. We can only hope."

He makes a fist, punching it into his flattened hand to crack his knuckles. He continues his terrifying rundown of the crimes, much as I wish he wouldn't. "Have you ever seen a broadhead arrow tip? It's like three razor blades, Mrs. Spencer. I've heard with deer, it feels like a shaving cut...just a neat slice. But the internal damage is irreparable. They drown in their own blood. Who could imagine killing just one person that way? And there were eight bodies buried out there. This woman made nine."

He finally registers my look of horror. "Now listen, I've given you a whole lot to take in at once. You need to go home to that lawyer husband of yours. I know he's seen bad things and he'll know what to say."

My thoughts feel smashed and stuck together, like seeds in overripe melon pith. Nine women. Nine women in the backyard at my job. Thomas never saw anything like this.

"I don't want you sharing any details of what I've said. I've told you things for one reason, Mrs. Spencer. I need someone on the inside here, someone who already has a relationship with people. I heard how you flushed out that killer last year. That's the kind of thinker I need on my team. You don't strike me as a flake, a fake, or any other character I normally hunt down. You have a level head and I'm pretty sure you care for the families of these victims."

I nod weakly.

"We're going to find them and let them know about their loved ones. But your observations of people involved with the spa will help me narrow things down. I won't beat around the bush. This recent death seems to point to a serial killer, and I'm severely understaffed at the police station."

"I have a child!" I burst out.

"And I have children, too. But sometimes God fingers people who are in the position to help Him enact justice here on earth. I'll do my dead-level best to protect you."

A clear image of the murdered woman floats into my mind. Toothy, open smile. Long, dark hair. Black leather everything. She was probably Nikki Jo's age. If something like that happened to her...

"I'll do it, but I want to know any details you have on this killer. I can't go into this thing blind."

He gives me a half-smile. "When I know, you'll know."

"And...I want you to stop chewing." I have no idea where this bold request comes from, outside the fact that I think it's a gross and destructive habit.

The detective chuckles. "You drive a hard bargain, Mrs. Spencer. But my wife's been bugging me to quit too. We've got a deal."

We shake hands. His are calloused, speaking of hard outdoor labor, not shuffling paper. I get a brief image of him, camped in the woods out back, stalking a killer. I imagine this woodsman knows just about all there is to know about bowhunting. Then again, maybe that makes him a suspect.

9

~*~

Your mother came to visit, weeping and wailing and gnashing her teeth. She asked all kinds of nosy questions, like did I talk to you on the phone? (Of course not, it would only make things harder on you.) Do I think of her often? (Yes, but only in the worst way.) When could we reunite our family? (Never.)

She has let herself go, as I knew she would. She's probably eating chocolates from those drug-store candy boxes and watching soap operas. The poor woman has no life outside you. Honestly, some people just take up space on this planet and contribute nothing. Now you know why I'm such a staunch supporter of population control. If she doesn't watch out, she'll make herself too ugly to find a new husband when we divorce.

I realize I am rather blunt in my letters to you, but I know you have the mind of an adult and you can understand and handle these concepts.

I gave the dean my notice on Monday. I figured if the college doesn't appreciate me, they can learn to live without me next year. Don't worry, I'll find other work. At least you and I will always land on our feet.

As I shut down the computer and pack up to leave, Teeny wanders out. Detective Tucker has already returned to the back yard with his men. A couple units have arrived, bearing cameras and crime scene equipment. I'm sure they're going to transport the poor woman's body to the morgue today.

"What's going on with the police cars?" Teeny looms over my desk, flipping a key ring around his large finger.

"Another body." I don't plan to go into detail with Teeny, who's already on my suspect list due to his strange off-book appointments today. I have a lot to report to Dani and I wish he would just leave already. I don't like being alone with this giant, no matter how benign he might seem.

His eyes widen. He seems genuinely surprised. "But this place was supposed to be safe."

"I know what you mean. It seemed like the safest place in the world, all tucked into the woods on this mountain top. I figured working here would be low-key."

Teeny looks confused. "Okay, I'd better get on home."

Curiosity gets the better of me. "And where is your home, Teeny? Do you live in town?"

Buckneck is the only place that would warrant being called a "town" on this side of the mountain. Even though it's hardly a metropolis with around 1,000 residents, it does have its own newspaper and post office, so it must be legit.

"Not right in town. I live outside it, up Fever Lick Road with my mom."

So he's about fifteen minutes away, which is the same distance I drive to work. Interesting he lives with his mom, because he must be in his thirties.

"I see. Do you have any appointments tomorrow? You know it's almost July Fourth weekend."

Teeny shakes his head. "Today was all." He looks at me intently, like he's about to say something, then abruptly turns and stalks out the door. I can't figure that one out.

As if she read my mind, Dani's *Buffy* ringtone sounds. She'd probably laugh if she knew I'd assigned such a violent TV show to her peace-loving, hippy self.

"What's the latest? Do I need to come in? Things are nearly settled with my family." She sounds relieved, but she won't be for long.

"Yes, you'd better come over. The police are still here and Detective Tucker needs to talk to you."

"What's going on? Something new turn up?"

I explain everything to Dani, from the avaricious IT guy to Teeny's mysterious appointments to the dead woman out back. Strangely, she seems most appalled that Teeny was putting in hours on the down-low.

"Who came in to see him? What did they look like?"

"Just a bleach blonde cougar type. I missed the other one—must've been in the kitchen or somewhere. Anyway, like I was saying, the body was the woman who went missing from the truck stop—"

"I heard you. No sense traveling cross-country like that. What kind of woman does that alone? I can't believe she wasn't even carrying a weapon."

"Detective Tucker didn't say that. Maybe she was." I'm not impressed with Dani's lack of sympathy for the dead woman. Then again, maybe senseless death doesn't fit into her worldview.

"Please lock up and tell Detective Tucker I'll be over in an hour. Thanks for holding down the fort. I have one more huge favor to ask. Could you open up for the computer guy tomorrow? I'll come over after lunch."

"Dani, there's all this scandal swirling at your pool site and you've basically dropped off the face of the earth! I can't be in charge here. I'm a receptionist, for

Pete's sakes. What if Tawny shows up again?"

"Don't stress that. I promise I'll be there in the afternoon. It's just...family is more important than business."

I know next to nothing about Dani's family. She's mentioned a sister, I think. But I do understand her point and I can tell she doesn't want to elaborate on her family issues with me.

"All right. I'll open tomorrow. But speaking of family, Saturday I have to be at home with my in-laws, okay?"

"No problem. Thanks for understanding, Tess. You're a gem. I have no idea what I'd do without you...Teeny would never do all this for me."

Once again I wonder why Dani is taking Teeny's appointments so personally. Surely those two aren't dating?

Andrew's turquoise Karmann Ghia is neatly tucked in the driveway by the big house. Just like its owner, the car is impossible not to notice. Andrew is a Brad Pitt lookalike, but thankfully his looks aren't the only thing he has going for him.

Andrew bashes through the front door to greet me, toting a squealing Mira Brooke on his shoulders. Today he's wearing his ponytail in some kind of man-bun.

I give Andrew a quick hug, tapping at his hair. "New style?"

He smiles, passing my daughter over to me. Mira Brooke's blue-gray eyes don't leave Andrew's face and she tries to reach for it. "You like your Uncle Andrew, don't you, sweetie?"

"'Course she does. I'm a lovable guy. And this baby doll is my favorite niece."

"And your only niece. Is your mom in?"

"Sure thing. You know she's planning a proper Southern picnic for tomorrow. Potato salad, pork barbeque, coleslaw, deviled eggs—"

"Did you bring a girl?"

He grins. "Now what kind of question is that? You treat my dating life with such disdain. But yes, I brought a girl."

I sigh. Mira Brooke clutches my hair and burbles.

"I know what you're thinking. 'He's in his second year of college, when is he going to get serious?' Well, I think I have. This one is a winner, just you wait and see."

Petey charges out the door with Thor. The tiny canine terror circles my legs, yipping as if I'm a total stranger. Petey shoos him off. "Knock it off, Thor! Sorry, Tess. Oh, and Mom's waiting for you." He swoops over and gives Mira Brooke a kiss on the cheek.

I arch an eyebrow at Andrew. He arches one back at me, as if throwing down the gauntlet.

"Your girlfriend inside? I'll be delighted to meet her," I say.

"You'll like her." His smug look oozes confidence.

"Here's hoping."

Just as I figured, the tension in the kitchen weighs heavier than the humid air outside. I'm fairly sure Nikki Jo instructed Petey to send me in as soon as possible. She stands by the sink, furiously gutting boiled eggs. A sleepy-eyed girl who looks like she should be smoking in a French café gazes at me, finally fixating on the gun at my waist. Mira Brooke effectively unconcealed it by kicking my shirt to the side. I set her down to adjust my clothes, which aren't nearly as fashion-savvy as the calculated-mismatched look Andrew's girlfriend is sporting.

Nikki Jo turns, hands covered in sticky yellow. "Oh honey child! So good to see you!" She tends to make a big deal of me in front of Andrew's girlfriends. "And Stella, this is Tess."

"Hi, Stella. Nice to meet you."

"Stella's staying with my friend Winnie Mae from church. Although I don't know if you go to church, do you, Stella?"

Stella shakes her head. "Religion is for the weak."

Nikki Jo turns back to the sink—doing an admirable job of tongue-biting.

"I just got back into church myself," I offer. "It's actually been really helpful. And I'm not weak."

She looks at my gun again. "I would guess you're not."

I sense that the snark factor is strong in this one. "Nikki Jo, would you mind watching Mira Brooke a little later on tonight? Like maybe around six?"

She washes her hands, drying them on a red towel that matches the Fourth of July decorations throughout the house. "You don't have to ask twice. You and Thomas going out?"

"No, just having a home-date."

"You want me to send food over?"

"No need, Thomas is picking up something. Thanks, Mom."

"How's the investigation?" The way she says it, you'd think I was lead detective on the case.

I have to tread carefully, since I don't want anything to leak before Detective Tucker gives the okay.

"They have some new evidence." I think a dead body could broadly be termed "evidence."

"Well, good. Leave it to Zeke to crack this thing wide open."

I nod, scooping up Mira Brooke.

Nikki Jo pipes up. "Listen, on your way out, could you tell Andrew to come in here? I need to ask him something." I suspect this is another ruse so she doesn't have to make conversation with Stella the sulky.

"I might could do that for ya." I hug Nikki Jo. "I'll bring her over in a couple hours. That way I'll have a little time with her today."

"You're a good mother, Tessa Brooke. Isn't she, Stella?"

My cheeks flame. My own mom never bragged on me like Nikki Jo and I never know the proper way to react.

Stella sniffs and jerks her head my way, like a queen trying not to notice a peasant.

Definitely time for me to leave. I really hope Thomas has something agreeable to discuss, or else this day is going to end even worse than it began.

10

I have applied for so many jobs and the response is always "You're overqualified." I tell them "Better overqualified than underqualified," but they usually show me the door. I would work in a McDonald's if I had to, but the local one isn't hiring since teens on summer break commandeered all the positions.

Hard to believe you're a teenager. I'm sorry I forgot your birthday but these dates are so trivial in the grand scheme of things, wouldn't you say? I hope your new foster family celebrated with you. Just look at it this way: every year is one year closer to sixteen, when I will bring you to live with me. And we'll hunt! Don't forget to keep practicing. I know I harp on this, but I would hate for your natural talent to go to waste.

You've always been quite gifted. Be sure to read extensively, on top of your school assignments. I'd love to discuss philosophers or poets with you when we meet again.

By the time Thomas gets home, I've changed to my favorite light blue pajamas and cut up a salad to go with our subs. A freshly-bathed Mira Brooke is safely ensconced with my in-laws for the evening. I can't imagine Stella spending any time with our little munchkin, but I have been pleasantly surprised by Andrew's girlfriends before.

After a quick peck, Thomas goes up to our room to change and unload his Smith & Wesson .45. When he comes downstairs in his plaid pj pants and tank T-shirt, I can't take my eyes from his gold-tan skin.

I squeeze his bicep. "Woah, baby. You been working out?"

He gives me a wink. "Trying to. I hate to say this, but maybe we'd better eat and talk first. But after that...who knows?" He pulls me into a tight hug and gives me a full, sensual kiss that leaves my lips tingling. "I just know you'll want to be aware of what's going on."

I slowly pull out of his embrace. "What's going on? Uh-oh. Is this heavy stuff? You'd better start talking."

As we get our food and settle on the couch,

Thomas tells me he's been offered the county prosecuting attorney position. The job opened sooner than expected because the current prosecutor died of a heart attack yesterday and he was only elected last year. There are three and a half more years left of his term.

"Tess, you know how we've been praying for direction for me? I feel like God is dropping this in my lap. I know it'll be a longer commute, but it's hardly grueling."

"Oh, honey! This would be amazing. How's the pay? The hours?"

The more Thomas tells me, the more I'm in awe. I've been praying for a new job for him, but didn't really believe anything would come through. A dark voice inside me says this only happened because Thomas was praying for it. When he prays, mountains seem to move. When I pray, things tend to get worse. Or—even more unbearably—nothing happens at all. I should probably start praying for patience, on top of a healthy dose of faith.

We celebrate by cracking open a bottle of sparkling cider left over from Mira Brooke's first birthday party. I fill Thomas in on the latest happenings at the Crystal Mountain Spa, including my decision to spy for Detective Tucker. He scrunches his eyebrows together, trying to reconcile the notion of me throwing myself in danger's path with his desire to look good for

Detective Tucker. My safety wins out.

"You don't have to do this. Shoot, let him ask Dani. She doesn't have kids. To be honest, I don't care if you never go back to work there. All that Yanni music and henna tattoos and orange peel massages."

I laugh. "There are no orange peel massages, silly. Bamboo, but not orange peel." I rub his shoulders. "I feel like I should help. This psycho is targeting women, and one of them was your mom's age."

"And they could be your age, too. You're right up in the epicenter, where all the bodies are. This feels creepy and all wrong."

I take our dishes over to the dishwasher and load some decaf coffee in our French press. Thomas is right about one thing—something is all wrong. I can't put my finger on it, but things aren't what they seem at the Crystal Mountain Spa.

After I tuck Mira Brooke in bed, Thomas heads over to the big house to visit with Andrew and Stella. I'm in the middle of *Rear Window* when Dani calls. Between the luminous, well-costumed perfection of Grace Kelly and the relentless plotline, I'm a sucker for this movie.

"I talked with Detective Tucker today. I'm getting a modified work schedule together. We'll talk about it tomorrow afternoon. You want to bring your suit and get some laps in? I know you love swimming and we'd have the pool to ourselves. I could fire up the sauna, too. I need to sweat out all this stress."

Dani knows me well. I love swimming, any time of day, any temperature pool. As a teen, I escaped to the outdoor pool near our trailer park every chance I could. I learned the easiest way to adjust to the ever-chilly water was to dive in and swim as if my life depended on it. Not a bad life philosophy, come to think of it.

"Sure. Will do. Thanks. I'll be glad to see you." Silence falls on the other end. "Dani? You there?"

"Sorry, yes. I'm here. Just have a lot on my mind and I don't want anyone else to get—"

"I know. Me neither. Well, I'll watch your back, and you watch mine." There's another pause. "Or not," I joke.

"No, Tess, I promise I'll have your back. See you tomorrow."

Velvet stalks my feet as I make coffee, and I wish I could sit on the couch with the kitty and savor the morning. I don't want to wake Mira Brooke, who finally tossed into a sweat-coated sleep somewhere around 3 a.m. We need to bite the bullet and buy an air-conditioner unit for these sweltery summer nights. Our little cottage is far from climate-controlled, with its hit-and-miss insulation and old windows. But it's bigger than a trailer and it's set on the ground. What more could a girl ask?

I rub frizz control serum on my hair, since the humidity charges its straight texture with a bit of unwanted oomph. I've let my short bob grow out to my shoulders and I can't tell if Thomas likes it this length. He's pretty enigmatic about his hair preferences, but seems to like just about anything I do, as long as I keep it brown.

I remember my mom growing her hair out nearly to her waist, saying "men like it better this way." I wish she'd spent less time trying to please men who didn't love her. Probably one of those leeches got her into selling prescription meds and then fled the scene when she got hauled off to prison.

Feeling festive for the Fourth, I pick out some denim trouser pants and a red paisley blouse that will cover my Glock. I roll Mira Brooke up into my arms, grab her diaper bag, and head up to the big house. She'll probably snuggle up with Nikki Jo for a little extra sleep.

By the time I get to the spa, not only Byron's van, but two police cars and a sedan with painted rust spots sit in the parking lot. Tawny Creeden steps out, all business in a boxy nineties suit.

"Mrs. Spencer. I hoped I would run into you. We need to talk."

Byron lounges in an Adirondack chair on the front porch. He proffers an encouraging wave. Who knows how long he's been here? He's either an early bird or voraciously nosy.

I speed-walk to the front door, planning to unlock it, zip inside, and lock it again—with or without Byron. I should leave him outside with the intrepid reporter. I still don't believe there's any serious computer work left to do.

As I insert the key, Tawny gets desperate and grabs my sleeve. I place my hand on my gun so she doesn't accidentally touch that next. Her eyes widen and she steps back.

I smile. "Miss Creeden. As I recall, both my boss and the lead detective said we are not at liberty to discuss this case."

Tawny tugs at one of her naturally ombré strands of hair, processing my comment. "So you're saying the case is still ongoing?"

I'll give her that much. "Yes. So you need to leave."

She glances at Byron, who's scrolling up his phone screen, effectively ignoring us. "Right, sure. I might just stay here in the parking lot until the detective comes out, though. Would that be okay?"

If she wants a run-in with Detective Tucker, I'll leave her to it. "Knock yourself out."

"Thanks." She strides off, her obviously-new heels slipping and flapping at the gravel. That girl has some courage, I'll give her that. Probably par for her job.

Byron springs into action, stashing his phone in his fitted jacket pocket and grabbing his messenger bag. Is it just me or does he look all dressed up today?

He grins. "Close encounter, eh?"

"I didn't think you were aware of what was going on, with your nose buried in that phone."

"I'm hurt, Tess."

I don't like the way he says my name. I fumble at the lock a moment longer than I should. When I flip the lights, I glance around the cozy wood interior of the reception room that feels strangely sterile. I'm starting to miss Dani's candlelit, musical ambiance in here. Besides, I had just about memorized all the lyrics to Enya's songs, even the unintelligible ones.

Byron starts chattering as I type in the computer password. "Read any great books lately? Call me a lightweight, but I just discovered Wodehouse and I can't get enough Jeeves and Wooster. Classics in their own right, wouldn't you say?"

"Sure. I actually prefer my classics on the lighter side, like Hawthorne or Hardy." I wait, wondering if he'll pick up on my irony or if he's a rehearsed fake.

He laughs. "Light like your Plath obsession, eh?"

So he does know his classics. But I still feel this guy is hiding something. Maybe he's Canadian with that "eh," but that's hardly the kind of secret I'm worried about.

Detective Tucker ambles down the hallway, giving Byron a once-over before motioning to me. I follow him back to the hair salon, our unofficial war room. The police must be working fast if he already has news on the body. He doesn't even have to say what he's thinking, because it's written all over his face: the killer will probably strike again soon.

11

~*~

I got hired today, working as a stocker at Woolworth's. I'm not sure about working for a woman boss, but Julie seems reasonably well-educated. I am going to try to fit in at my first blue-collar job. I've even bought some T-shirts and jeans—can you imagine? Even when I hunt I wear old khakis so it is definitely a stretch for me. I'll be in the back room all the time, never out on the sales floor when people are around. I like to think of myself as a hidden treasure. Maybe I'll work my way up.

Your new foster family never writes to me, like Karen did. I wonder how she is doing. Do you ever speak with her? She wasn't married, was she? That would explain her naïveté about married relationships like your mother's and mine. But she saw your potential, and for that I'm grateful. I hope the family you are with now appreciates you.

I have actually moved into Hope's Grove

Commune, where we share income, grow our own food, and support one another in tangible ways. I don't think you have written me lately, but please note the new address on the envelope for future reference. Don't worry. By the time you come to live with me, I will have saved up enough for an apartment again, though perhaps you would enjoy commune life. Your mother would deem it wildly inappropriate, the way both genders network and mesh around here.

I am, by nature, a more reticent person, but I have found that I have been able to contribute to the greater good many times, even if it's just sharing a lesson in philosophy when people gather around the fire pit at night. I think many happy memories will be made here at Hope's Grove.

Detective Tucker brings me up to date on the investigation. "The arrow is nondescript—just a regular carbon arrow, could have been bought anywhere in the country. But we're finding out more about the skeletons." He pauses, probably not sure I want to hear more.

"Go on," I encourage, bracing my stomach for more gruesome news.

"These women had been reported missing, from

various states, starting about twenty-four years ago. Most—but not all—of them were married, white, aged anywhere from twenties to fifties. No unifying hair color, size, or job, so that's not our link. But there's always a link with these serial killers, even if they're trying to be random. Something always drives them to choose who they do, even if it's only because that person seems like an easy target."

"That motorcyclist seemed very independent and she was separated from her husband."

"Good thought. We'll check up on the separation angle. Not sure how to establish what their dispositions were, but we'll talk to some of the remaining husbands. You're right, though, it could be a personality trait that drew him. And I'm saying 'him,' but I'm not entirely sure it's a man yet."

"Aren't serial killers usually men?" I seem to recall that from CSI shows.

"Usually. But not universally. I've heard male and female serial killers often have different motivations. All the more reason to try and understand the link between these victims." He works his mouth, but there's no chew in it. He sighs, pulls a piece of bright green gum from his pocket, and pops it in. "That's all I have now. I filled Ms. Gibson in on the bodies yesterday, since it's her spa and her decision if she wants to close it up for a while. She's not married, is she?"

Somehow, I've never gotten around to discussing Dani's dating life with her. She appears very transparent, offering up tidbits about her healthy eating habits, her dreams for the spa...but when I ask personal questions, she changes topic so cleverly, I never even know she's doing it.

"I don't think so. I'll find out, maybe today after work."

"Right. Well, this will be my last day officially on-site. The bodies are in the medical examiner's office, and I'm just supervising the final clean-up. I'll stake out the woods on my own time. But for now, I want you staying out of them. Park as close to the building as possible. Also, try to leave with someone every day. Don't be alone—even though I know you're carrying."

"Is it that obvious?"

"You walk a little stiffer with that gun on you. Try to pretend like it's part of your body."

I feel self-conscious, like a total newbie. "Thanks. Will do."

"That Byron out there interests me. He keeps showing up here early. You heard of criminals who inject themselves into the investigation? Return to the scene of the crime, that kind of thing? He gets my dander up."

"Me too. I'll let you know if he says anything."

Detective Tucker and I nod at each other and split up in the hallway. A flicker in the massage room draws me to it—did Teeny show up again and light candles? When I push open the door and turn on the light, the room looks empty. Great, now I'm seeing things.

Byron is still set up at my computer. As I walk in, he catches my eye. "Tess, could you come here a second?" He points at the screen as I come closer. "See this? This is what has taken all my time."

Even as he tells me what I'm looking at, I get the strong impression he's lying just to get me to stand next to him. I should have read up on computer lingo and whipped out some of that to shut him down faster.

At the conclusion of his monologue, he gives me a brilliant smile. "So that's what I was dealing with and I'm all finished. I think we need a drink, you and I. This has been a truckload of work and I know everyone else is off."

Those last words send a shiver down my arms. "Actually, I don't drink. And I'm meeting someone here today."

His smile wavers. "Surely we could do something to celebrate? Any food in that kitchen back there?"

As he loads his things, I notice again how fitted his clothes are, making it clear he must work out like a maniac. He's probably quite strong, which isn't comforting in the least. I don't like his familiarity with this building, much less his suggestion we scrounge up a celebratory lunch. He's pushing himself at me.

"No, I don't think my boss would appreciate that.

She'll be here soon. In fact, you might want to explain those repairs to her, so she's ready for the bill." I give a short laugh.

He looks genuinely disappointed, like a child who didn't receive the one Christmas present he begged for. "Of course I'd do that, but I should get back to the office before *my* boss calls. Are you ever in town?"

I point to my ring finger. "Married. So I would never be in town with you."

Byron finally seems to take the hint, but as he brushes past me, his fingers catch my arm and he whispers in my ear. "Should you ever want to talk sad poets, Tess Spencer, you know where to find me."

He adjusts his glasses, leveling a suggestive blue gaze at me, which I try to return in daggers. I watch out the window until his van slowly pulls away. The police cars have gone, as has Detective Tucker's distinctive Hummer. The only car in the lot is my red SUV.

I move away from the windows, dropping into an oversized leather chair in the corner. I take my Glock out and set it on the table next to me, aimed at the front door. One thing's for doggone sure: if that killer shows up here, I'm not going down without a fight.

12

The female psyche is indeed a mystery best not pondered by the male gender. From the pot-sotted women in the commune to Julie at work, I'd rather avoid them altogether. One thing is screaming obvious: they are all so needy. Julie tries to domineer over me like a mother hen. The commune women are desperate for any male attention, which I find revolting. Your mother wasn't the only one of her kind, it would seem.

I find myself daydreaming about the soft leaves and the earthy smell of my great-grandpa's land. That moment of decision before I let the arrow fly. That tang of deer blood spilled on the snow. Hunting is cathartic.

I am trying to show compassion toward these women, to focus inward with my meditation and not allow their behavior to undermine my happiness. Sometimes I think being antisocial is the only way to achieve nirvana. Buddha must not have been surrounded by women.

Dani unlocks the door right after I text Thomas to see if he'll be home in time for his Mom's picnic tonight. I'll be glad to have some down-time with the Spencer family, even though I'll probably need to make polite small-talk with Stella.

Today, Dani sports a flowing blouse, buttery-looking ankle boots, and stick-straight jeans. Her oversized hoop earrings, Chanel tote, and loose braid complete the look—a look I could never put together in my wildest imaginings. Some women are born with fashion sense, some regret not having it, and some don't care. I fall into the middle category.

She ignores me as I sheathe the Glock. "Time for a swim? I thought you'd be ready to roll." She strips off her gorgeous outfit, right down to a navy bandeau swimsuit that probably cost over two hundred dollars.

"Sorry. I'll go change in the dressing room. Dani, you've got to talk with this computer guy. I really think he's giving you the runaround."

She shoves her boots and clothes into the seemingly bottomless black tote. "I really don't want to talk about it yet. Honestly, I need to cleanse myself of all this negative energy and I think the pool and sauna are the way to go. I'll fire up the sauna while you change."

I don my orchid lap suit and store my gun in a spa locker, which is wood-paneled and stocked with peppermint shampoo, cocoa body butter, and a thick white bath robe. I don't know how Dani afforded this kind of luxury, but people will come from quite a distance to experience it. A log cabin this spa's size would have bankrupted most people around here.

In the pool room, Dani cuts a flawless backstroke toward the deep end. My backstroke looks more like I'm flailing for my life. I squeeze on my swim cap, snap on my goggles, then dive in and commence my overhand stroke. The nice thing about this pool is that it has extended, marked lap lanes. We swim in silence for about ten minutes, then she pauses, draping her arms over the mosaic tiles. I pull up at the opposite wall and wait.

"Everything is convoluted," she says.

I nod, trying to listen more than speak. Sometimes it's an effort for me.

"I moved here to find peace and quiet. To find harmony in nature and in humans. Rural living should be closer to perfection, I would think."

"Adam and Eve came from the Garden of Eden and one of their sons murdered the other." I grip the pool's edge, treading water. "There's no perfection on earth, doesn't matter where you live. We do notice the bad things faster in a tight rural community. Difference is, we rally around each other because we're related or we've grown up together."

"Or maybe you just care more," she muses.

"To be honest, much of the compassion you find in Buckneck comes from Christians. Yes, there's sometimes judgment passed along with the gossip. But in the end, we support each other, because no one's perfect and we all fall on hard times now and again."

She nods. "I've decided to close the salon for a month. I won't have all those clients around if there's a killer up here. Or is he up here, Tess? I don't know. Why would someone choose this spot to bury women? Were they trying to shut me down?"

I hadn't thought of that angle. "Who knows? But I think that's a great idea. What about Teeny? And your henna and spa treatments?"

"We could keep those up, just the three of us. But are you up for manning the front desk?"

I nod, because I've committed to Detective Tucker, not because of any strong motivation to work.

Dani smiles, and I'm hit with an unexpected wave of protectiveness toward this enigmatic woman who's been so beleaguered in our small town.

"You want to hit the sauna? Should be toasty by now." I suggest it because I know she wants to unwind and maybe she'll continue opening up...not because I want to go in there.

Even in the extra-roomy sauna, with its blue recessed lighting, my claustrophobic tendencies kick in the minute the door thuds closed. I have to will them away by singing something utterly distracting in my head, such as "Battle Hymn of the Republic" or "Mr. Tambourine Man." My penchant for Bob Dylan songs stymies Thomas as much as it does me.

Once we're settled in the dim light, I imagine the cozy warmth permeating my skin, my bones. I try to breathe evenly. I think about those bones out back...bodies swaddled under that dark soil for years, while their family and friends longed for closure.

Dani seems to follow my thoughts. "Detective Tucker didn't tell me how the women were killed. Said that's under investigation. Do you know?"

I don't like lies, but sometimes I have to reword the truth. "I don't know all the details."

She sighs. "Seems like if there's a serial killer, we need to know how they're killing, wouldn't you say? I know you have a gun." She winks and I stiffen, surprised she noticed. She continues. "But some of us don't. I want to know what I'm up against."

I understand Dani's feeling, but I can't share anything Detective Tucker has deliberately kept from her. Word could leak out to the press.

I jump up. I totally forgot about Tawny!

"What's wrong?" Dani leans forward.

"Tawny Creeden came by this morning,

determined to get a scoop. She said she'd wait around for Detective Tucker. I didn't see her leave, but her car was gone when the repairman left. I should have checked on her." A premonition sweeps over me. "I need to call Detective Tucker and see if she caught up with him."

Water droplets sizzle on the hot coals as I walk to the door to retrieve my phone. When I twist the knob, the door doesn't give. I try again, shoving at it. Panic threatens to choke me. "Is there a lock on this door?"

"Yes, there's a high slide lock to keep children out when no one's around. Wait—you mean it's locked?" Dani rushes to my side, helping me push at the door. Her blue eyes widen. "I left my phone out in my bag, too!"

"And my Glock's in the locker." I sag onto the bench, the weight of the heat and the windowless room pressing on me. No amount of singing is going to get me through this.

13

I suppose there are some things about marriage I miss, like hot meals on the table when I get home from work, or someone to care when I don't show up on time. But I am a person who values individual freedom and I've never liked being closely monitored like that.

There's a girl in our commune who calls herself Sea, but of course that's a trumped-up name if ever I've heard one. She was waiting for me one day when I got back to the central house. It's a large building where we eat together and have a shared bathroom and shower area. Anyway, she's probably twenty years younger than I am and quite clueless about what to do with her life. She served up a bowl of tofu stew she had cooked (to be honest, it turned my stomach), and she asked me some big questions, like what is the purpose of suffering, what happens when we die, and more. Apparently someone had told her I'm a philosophy professor.

After spending about an hour talking her through things, I felt lonelier than ever. I wished I could share my insights with you. I feel so much of my wisdom will be lost to the sands of time that separate us. I tell you all this so you know I do miss you and think of you often. No matter what your mother tells you, remember that.

The stuffiness in the room seems to siphon air from my lungs, like a parasite. I might die in here, without saying goodbye to Thomas or Mira Brooke or my family. My arms start shaking and I crunch over on the bench.

Dani takes the fire poker and tries wedging it near the lock. She glances back at me.

"Tess, hang in there. I forgot you're claustrophobic. Want to talk about that?"

"No." My voice comes out in an unfamiliar croak.

Dani keeps talking as she jiggers the poker. "I have a touch of arachnophobia, and where I grew up there were some pretty huge spiders. I'm talking tarantulas. Well, one night I woke up and found one crawling on my shoulder. I decided I'd had it with my fear. I got up, turned on the light with the spider still on me, casually flicked it to the floor, and then *made myself* pick it up. Of course, it was stunned, so it wasn't super-active. But I learned I didn't have to fear them. Not that I didn't have the overwhelming urge to stomp it into oblivion." She drops the poker near the coals and sighs. "This isn't going to work."

I register everything Dani is saying, but I won't be distracted by talk of spiders. I can't tear my eyes from the solid walls, which seem to be getting tighter. If only I had my Glock—so help me I would blow that door off its hinges.

Dani prowls around the sauna, searching for something to get us out. "Really, we'll be okay. The coals are cooling off. We have that decorative waterfall unit over there...we could drink that water if we got desperate. All we need to stay alive for several days is air and water, you know."

How does a city girl like Dani know all these random survival facts? Even though she's speaking reason, my mind and body have gone beyond that point, into the realm of *this will kill me.*

"So, tell me how you and Thomas met," she says.

My brain whirs and fills in the memory. "I had moved to Buckneck with Miranda." I focus on Dani's tan face and her half-smile.

"Miranda," she repeats, as if it's a magic word.

"My mother went to prison," I continue.

Her half-smile tightens, flattens to a grimace. "Go

on."

"I moved out, worked for a little consignment shop. Met Thomas' mom there. She went home and told him about this 'cute little brunette'...and the rest is history."

Dani's pale blue eyes pull me in, lined flawlessly in rich brown. Her champagne eye-shadow and bronzer catch the dim light and shimmer. Even as I wonder how she gets her hair that perfect shade of streaky blonde, my eyes travel to the locked door. My mind snaps back into fear mode and I suck at air like I'm drowning. I can't even pretend to be chill in this situation.

What if Dani had someone lock us in on purpose? What if she's the serial killer? I study her face for signs of guilt and her eye twinges. I will my hand to form a fist, but can't get my arm to follow-up and punch her.

"Another thing." Her voice is soothing and she moves to the bench behind me. "I was in the Marines. You'd never know it, would you? And I learned a little trick." In one swift move, her arm locks around my neck. I hear her say "chokehold." All the colors fade to black and white, and then I'm out.

When I come to, Dani's taking apart the water unit. Who is this woman?

I groan from the bench, where she's stretched me out. "What the *stink* did you do that for?" I ask.

She glances at me. "I could tell you were freaked out of your mind and planning to hit me. Knowing your phobia, you might have started flailing around and knocked the one composed person in this room senseless. I just got to you first. Now *please* lie there and don't move. I plan to get us out of here somehow."

"By disassembling the water feature?"

"Maybe I can get some pressure built up, then redirect the water flow toward the lock and blow it."

"Are you serious? Do you know what you're talking about or just making it up from a *MacGyver* episode?"

She shoots me a glare. "Have a little faith in me."

I have to admit that Dani has provided a major focal point for my anxiety. Now I'm more stressed about what she'll do next than the possibility of dying in this locked sauna.

"No...wait..." She pulls wires and tubing as she talks herself through it. "This should go here..."

"How about we try smashing through again? Maybe we didn't ram it hard enough."

"What did I say? You have to—"

A click interrupts her. Someone's shoving the lock back. Dani drops everything, grabbing the poker faster than I can say *scat*. She's at my side, poker raised, when the door opens.

The person standing on the other side does not compute in my fear-fogged brain.

Towering man with white-blond hair, chiseled chin, and muscles not even vaguely hidden by his green polo shirt. Thick German accent as he says, "Tess Spencer. Now I have found you."

Before I can say a word, Dani swings at him like a wildcat in a cage. He catches the poker with one hand. He could probably bend it in two if he wanted.

Axel Becker, enigmatic local florist and my personal college stalker, has walked back into my life.

14

Your mother found out I work at Woolworth's and came to visit, bearing what I assume was a conciliatory loaf of banana walnut bread. I do not want to make up and make nice. This is a separation, the point being that we stay separate.

I will make this short, but do not tell her where I am living. I know she'd probably never darken the door at Hope's Grove Commune, but you never know. She is furious she can't visit you. Of course you might sentimentally want to see her again, but you need to understand mothers don't always know best. Sometimes fathers do. I will lie low and write again in a few months. In the meantime, don't tell anyone where I am.

Axel doesn't seem fazed in the least after being attacked by a swimsuit-clad woman. He opens the door wide so we can both exit. Dani refuses to go anywhere near him, standing her ground in the sauna. He remains silent, assuming I'll explain.

It's tricky, because I don't know much about Axel except that he shows up at opportune times and has a knack of saying remarkable things to me. Also, he happens to be the most incongruous florist I'll ever meet. But given the savage look in Dani's eyes, which doesn't jibe at all with my surfer-girl image of her, I'd better talk fast. I walk out of the room that has become my worst nightmare and into the fresh air of the hallway.

"Don't worry, I know him. Axel Becker, owner of Fabled Flowers over in Point Pleasant. We went to the same college in South Carolina. Although I don't know how he got into the spa."

Dani nods furiously. "Yes. Kindly explain how and why you came in here, Axel Becker."

Axel's voice is calm and deep. "Tess works here. I saw the car that is hers. I knocked but heard no answer. Around the building I walked, and came through the door by your pool for swimming." His German accent gets more pronounced the longer he speaks.

"Someone left the back door open? I know I locked it. This doesn't make sense." Dani stalks past Axel and retrieves her phone from her tote. I figure she's calling Detective Tucker.

Axel's whole story is suspicious. Maybe he was the one who locked us in. But why would he let us out? I glare at him. "Why were you following me all the way up here?"

Axel gestures toward the reception room. "Come, sit."

"Hang on a minute. I have to get my things first." I go to the locker room to change and strap on my gun, which gives me no small measure of relief.

So much for Detective Tucker's empty promise to keep me from danger. I suppose this was partly my fault. I didn't check the back door. I didn't bring my gun into the sauna. I let my phobia get the better of me. Right now I feel utterly defeated. I should probably quit my job and stay home with my daughter, which is what I'd rather do—just forget about Thomas' student loan payments. But again, the dead woman's words sound in my ears as if she were standing right here. She bravely chased after a better life, only to die in the process. I don't want to see any other women die.

When I meet Axel in the reception room, he begins to explain. "Upon my return from Germany, I wanted to review the latest happenings. In the news article on the Crystal Mountain Spa, I observed that you were an employee. Today I wanted to offer floral decoration for the interior, if the owner showed interest."

I had forgotten *The Buckneck Daily* did a news feature on the spa last year. Tawny didn't cover it, but the reporter who did couldn't write worth a lick. On top of that, our staff picture was so pixelated it was barely recognizable. Axel must have been using a magnifying glass to figure out it was me. Still, I think I believe him. He helped me out last year when I was tracking a killer.

Dani stalks in, fully dressed and talking up a blue streak on her phone. I should call Thomas or try and get home. I think I can drive, but I still feel woozy even while I'm sitting down.

From the sound of things, Dani isn't talking with Detective Tucker, but rather reaming Teeny out.

I look up into Axel's concerned eyes. "You'll have to ask Dani about the flowers. I appreciate your help, but I need to go home. I have a daughter now—Miranda Brooke."

"Miranda Brooke Spencer." He smiles. "It is blessed that you are given this child. I will send flowers."

I shake my head. Thomas doesn't care for Axel, to put it mildly. "No need for flowers. By the way, when did you come back from Germany?"

He hesitates only slightly, then says, "This past month."

Dani drops her phone into her tote, then stares blankly out the window.

"Perhaps I could provide flowers for this spa,"

Axel says to her back.

She turns, obviously not registering his words. "Yes...maybe. Tess, could you call Detective Tucker? I don't have his number."

"Sure. Didn't you call him? Or did you just talk with Teeny?"

"Only to Teeny." She changes the subject. "I'll close up. Why don't you wait at your car for me? Then we'll leave at the same time." She ignores Axel.

"Of course." I start to stand and wobble a bit. Axel extends his hand, helping me up. He doesn't creep me out the way Byron does for some inexplicable reason.

He pushes open the door and walks in front of me to the SUV. I feel shielded because if a rogue bowhunter is trying to take a shot, the arrow would have to go through Axel first. I don't even think it could. The man seems like he's sculpted from marble.

I unlock my SUV door and Axel opens it. As I settle into the driver's seat, concern etches his brow. "What happened in the heated room, Tess? Did the woman Dani hurt you?"

The protective tone in his voice comes through loud and clear. If I answer *yes*, it might be like unleashing my own personal guard dog. I don't think we need to get that drastic. But the whole sauna experience was baffling. Did someone know I was claustrophobic? Did Teeny have something to do with it? Did Dani have to put me in a chokehold?

I shake my head, coming back to how Dani tried to talk me through my fear, how determined she was to get us out of the sauna. She was just as surprised as I was to be locked in there. "No, she didn't hurt me. She tried to help me."

Axel nods curtly, scanning the woods and spa as if sensing the tainted vibes. He should probably be aware of this murderer on the loose. "There is a serial killer running around here somewhere," I say.

He nods again.

I repeat myself. "Did you hear me? A serial killer—a person who has killed several people?" I explain, in case his German is the problem.

"I know of this," he says, still scanning.

How does he know when it hasn't even come out in the news yet? I'm probably a fool for trusting him. His entire demeanor screams "sleeping lion," and yet my gut instinct says this lion would never turn on me.

Dani emerges from the building, her usual confident stride downgraded to a half-hearted stalk. She goes straight to her sleek Honda coupe and waves at us before tearing out of the parking lot. She's ticked, all right. She might be going to accost Teeny right now. As well she should, if he was the one who locked us in.

It's difficult to have a conversation with Axel, and right now I need to call Detective Tucker. He might be able to make sense of things.

"*Vielen dank*, Axel." My college German is rusty

but I still remember a few basic phrases.

He smiles and it feels like sunlight beaming on me. "*Immer.*" Always.

As he walks to his older black Mercedes, I pull away, pondering. I'm fairly certain Axel was lying when he said he only returned to West Virginia last month. But I'm not going to question the one God sent to unlock that sauna door. I'm going to figure out who locked it in the first place.

15

I've gone two months without seeing her, then tonight she showed up in the parking lot and tried to follow me home. I finally lost her with some skillful car maneuvering, but the point is that your mother is getting to be a pain.

Also, Julie at work asked if I wanted to join her at Cecile's Restaurant after work. Can you believe it? A woman asking a man on a date is ridiculous. If I wanted to go on a date, I would have asked her. And Sea is always pointing to me, tittering away at the commune as if I'm invisible. I don't know what I said, but she seems to have it in for me.

Meanwhile, besides helping with the communal garden, I usually mellow out by reading. So far this summer, I've read through Nietzsche's The Birth of Tragedy *and Thoreau's* On Walden Pond. *Yes, I confess I've never read that, even though I should have.*

Altogether I cannot complain. I am just having difficulty living in the "now" when all these women toss me about like waves, toying with my emotions. I came here for introspection, and sadly I have had little time to practice it.

I pull in at The Buckneck Daily, a nondescript brick building you wouldn't know was a newspaper office, save for a drooping, stencil-lettered sign over the door.

A disinterested secretary mans the desk, barely glancing up at me, even though I'm probably her only visitor today. She flicks a greasy piece of hair from her face, staring at a chunky desktop screen that must be ten years old.

"Excuse me. I'm looking for Tawny Creeden?"

That wakes her up. She nearly knocks over her oversized Mountain Dew. "What for?"

"She was researching a story and I didn't get to say goodbye. Just wanted to clear up a few details." That sounds better than "I wanted to make sure she got back alive."

"She ain't been in all day. Our boss ain't none too happy about it."

I nod, trying not to let apprehension creep into my voice. "Do you have some paper and a pen?"

She hands me a yellow sticky note and a permanent marker. I write my name and cell number, adding a smiley face for good measure. "Please tell her to call me as soon as she gets a chance."

The woman unabashedly picks up the note, reading my name aloud. "Tess Spencer. Any relation to that lawyer in town?"

"He's my husband." I'm not sure how this news will be received.

She merely huffs and sticks the note on her smudged computer screen. "I'll get it to Tawny, but if you see 'er first, you'd better call me here. You ain't never seen a rage till you seen Mr. Messer in one. She's his star reporter, too."

She shakes her head, clucking as I go out the door.

Back in my SUV, I call Detective Tucker. He finally picks up on the fourth ring. I briefly give him a rundown of the sauna debacle, including Dani's covert Marine skills, and ask him about Tawny.

"Did she catch you before you left?"

"Actually, I didn't leave. I parked my Hummer off-road and went up that back trail a ways. I've been camped here, watching the woods."

"You mean you were that close to the spa when we were locked in?"

"Trust me, I had no idea you were in trouble or I would've shown up. I wasn't watching the spa. I needed to know if someone has been visiting the woods. So far, no one has been here. Lots of trees that would be easy to climb up and sit in, though."

"Well, that's not comforting. Shouldn't we try to find Tawny? She drives a beat-up, rusty dark blue car."

"I'll tell police to keep an eye open, but we can't do much until she's reported missing. She married?"

"I'll check the phone book and ask around."

"I'm sorry you were trapped in there, Mrs. Spencer. You mentioned you were afraid of small spaces?"

"Yes." I really don't want to talk about my phobia.

"Then you ought to be aware of this: we're fairly certain the latest victim was stashed in the trunk of a car at some point, and forensics show some of the other women might have been, too. The killer may have abducted the women in the trunk, or toted them to the burial site in it. Point being, maybe you ought to read up on how to get out of a car trunk."

It takes a minute for that comment to register. "What? I thought you said you'd keep me safe!"

"I said I'd do my dead-level best to protect you. Sometimes that means you have to keep yourself safe. For instance, where was your Glock when you were in that sauna?"

I'm being scolded. My cheeks flame. "It was a sauna!"

His voice gentles. "Keep it on you at all times when you're at the spa. Even if you're with someone you know." Axel's face pops into my mind.

"I can do that."

"Okay. I need to stop talking out here in the open. Keep checking into Tawny and get back to me." He hangs up.

I finally head home, reluctant to gear up for Nikki Jo's Independence Day party tonight. I need to tell someone about the sauna lock-in, but I don't want to drop that bomb on Thomas. Finally, I call Charlotte on my speaker phone.

"Tess. Everything all right?"

"Not really." I have a sudden brainstorm. "Are you doing something tonight? Could you drop by this evening so we can talk, then join us for a Spencer family picnic? I know Nikki Jo won't mind."

"That would be great. I need to get out of this place for a while and I have nothing to do at home. Bartholomew's at a conference. What can I bring?"

Charlotte arrives as I'm bathing Mira Brooke. She takes over so I can change, not caring if her quilted gypsy skirt winds up looking like she just left a water park. When Charlotte unbuckles her cork wedges, I gasp.

"Those shoes are gorgeous! And look at your pristine coffee toenail polish. Girl, if I only had half your skill at accessorizing...or just looking swank in general."

Charlotte laughs as Mira Brooke squirts water at her dark hair, a perfect chocolate-cherry color.

"Tess, you always look swank...more like *glam*. You put on some lipstick and I swear you look like one of those fifties' movie stars. Now quit running yourself down and tell me what happened today."

Mira Brooke giggles in the tub, and a grassy-smelling, crickety breeze swirls through the bedroom window. I don't want to think about my claustrophobic sauna moments. But Charlotte might have some insight into the lock-in, so I fill her in.

"Wait—Dani Gibson put you in a headlock? And Axel showed up? Wasn't he the German who had a crush on you last year?"

"I wouldn't say *crush*. I mean he did stalk me in college and steal a kiss there. But I don't think he feels that way about me now. I'll tell you who is disturbing—Byron, the computer guy."

"Right. Yeah, sounds like he was hitting you up what with all that touchy-feely stuff and asking to meet in town. What possessed him to ask a married woman on a date? Was he probing for information?"

"I figure he's angling to know something. Oh! And I didn't tell you about Tawny Creeden."

Mira Brooke offers a few parting splashes before Charlotte takes her from her bath seat, wrapping her in a towel. "What about Tawny? I think she went to my school."

I assemble and dismantle outfits as I explain. "She asked me about the bodies. When I refused to tell her anything, she waited in the parking lot to talk with Detective Tucker. But he said she never caught up with him, and her car was gone before Dani came."

A pair of white jeans and a navy striped tank finally seem to fit the bill, so I leave them on. Charlotte finagles a wiggly Mira Brooke into a diaper and a red romper.

"I'm worried about Tawny," I say.

"It is fishy." Charlotte snatches my new favorite perfume, *Very Irresistible* by Givenchy, and sprays me three times with it. Then she rummages through my drawer, unearthing a bright green collar necklace and cubic zirconia stud earrings. "Put these on," she commands.

Mira Brooke toddles after Charlotte to my closet and starts pulling my shoes out, one by one.

"Good girl—that's just what I needed." Charlotte winks. She matches up a pair of green ballet flats I forgot I owned and tosses them my way. "Now, hair and makeup."

By the time Charlotte's finished with me, I feel like a new woman. I don't want to worry about Tawny and Dani and Axel and Byron. I don't want to think of the dead woman's face and burial ground behind the spa.

Thomas comes home just as I'm making the sweet tea. He gives Charlotte a wave, Mira Brooke a smooch, and then stops and stares at me.

"Woah."

Charlotte grins and discreetly carries Mira Brooke out to the porch swing.

Thomas steps closer, tracing my cheek with his fingertips. "You look...like jailbait."

I tip up to give him a long kiss, losing most of my pink lip gloss. "Thanks, babe. You'd better get ready. Mom will be waiting."

"I can't even make casual conversation. You have derailed my brain. Unhinged? I can't think of the word."

My phone rings. "It's your Mom! Get ready because I know she doesn't want that barbeque to get cold. We'll go on over."

After assuring Nikki Jo we're on our way, I carry the tea and Charlotte walks Mira Brooke up our gravel path to the big house. Red and purple flowers tumble onto the pathway, a wondrous profusion Nikki Jo has tended to. Mira Brooke stops to sniff as many as she can, enchanted.

Although I tend to kill flowers, there's an antique rosebush I've been watering all summer and it seems determined to survive. It's finally blooming, its roses a dusty pink with apple green edging. Before the

Campbells' house sold, the Good Doctor—Bartholomew Cole—wanted me to have a keepsake of Rose. We dug up and transplanted this bush from her expansive rose garden, and every time I look at it, I'm flooded with memories. Above all, I feel awestruck that God protected me the last time I went to that house.

Charlotte catches my misty gaze as I touch the satiny rose petals. She gives me a half-hug as we come up to Nikki Jo and Roger's back yard.

It's more like a private paradise, the smooth circle of grass hedged in with large-leafed blue hostas and sprawling rhododendrons. A curtained pavilion is the latest addition to the bluestone patio. Nikki Jo runs out to hug Charlotte, always delighted to see Miranda's daughter.

Stella relaxes in one of the white rockers, looking sleek as a cat in a ruffly white blouse and black cigarette pants. Andrew does a goofy jig over to us and picks up Mira Brooke. When he spins her around, I gasp.

"Your hair! I didn't think you'd ever cut it." He's sporting a new layered haircut that makes his hair look even more blond. The ponytail is gone.

"Figured I might as well get all duded up for Mom's soirée." He winks at me before focusing on Charlotte. "And who is this exotic creature?"

Charlotte rolls her eyes. It's rare that two perfect specimens of humanity, like Charlotte and Andrew, are in such close proximity. You have the feeling they're on a collision course. They will inevitably be drawn to one another, like opposing magnetic poles. In this case, Charlotte is at least fifteen years older than Andrew, but something tells me that would only make her more of a challenge for him.

Petey chases Thor onto the patio, a welcome diversion. He got a haircut too, and looks older without his unruly mop of red curls. Hard to believe he'll be driving soon.

"Hey Tess, we need to do some shooting. On the range or video games—I don't care what. I just want to hang."

Thomas' hand falls on my shoulder, and I lean into him as he answers for me. "Let's go shooting tomorrow out on the property. Tess needs to practice with her new Glock. Andrew, you in? Would Stella want to join us? She could use Dad's little revolver."

Stella pipes up, setting her jadeite tumbler of sweet tea on the table, where I'm afraid the frolicking Thor will bump it. "I don't believe in violence of any kind."

Andrew grins and drops a kiss on her forehead. "Of course you don't, darling." He gives me a knowing look. "But sometimes the violence finds you, doesn't it? And we Spencers look after our own."

16

~*~

Today Julie scolded me publicly for ordering too many girdles for the floor. It was probably one of the most embarrassing moments of my life. When I was a professor, no one would have dared dress me down like that. I managed to keep quiet and take the verbal beating. Perhaps she is smarting because I turned her down on a date and she felt the need to put me in my place.

The problem is, my "place" in life is far advanced beyond hers. She is wallowing in ignorance. I would love to teach her to be careful with her words, to develop right speech. But she will have none of it, I am sure. She sees me only as a servant, slaving away for my paycheck.

I have deliberately taken time away from women, trying to sustain a celibate, unhindered thought life. And yet it seems at every turn, they inject themselves into my life in a very physical way. I don't know how much longer I can ignore their unkind words and unwanted advances.

Roger places Nikki Jo's jadeite platter, heaped with barbeque, in the middle of the table. Mira Brooke lurches for it, nearly slipping from my lap. Like the rest of us, this girl loves her grandma's food.

After Roger prays, we pass the seemingly endless parade of dishes, piling our plates full. I feed Mira Brooke while Thomas eats, then we'll trade off.

The conversation moseys around to how the town of Buckneck got its name. Charlotte is interested and Roger loves sharing the story, since it's his family that was involved.

"Back in the 1890s, not long after West Virginia became its own state, a family by the name of McBride lived in these parts. This was on my mother's Irish side. They had a son named Thomas McBride."

I glance at Thomas as he takes a gulp of fresh-squeezed lemonade. This story always mortifies him because his parents probably named him after Thomas McBride, now infamous in the oral history of the Spencer family. His tan face hides his embarrassed flush well, and when his hickory brown eyes meet mine, I give him a comforting wink.

"Our Tommy-boy obeyed his momma and didn't booze around or gamble. But one night, some disreputable friends slipped a little white lightning in his punch—moonshine, you know." Roger is just getting warmed up to the tale. Charlotte props her chin on her slim wrists, soaking up the details. Stella takes a dainty bite of potato salad and pays no attention.

"A fast game of poker commenced. Tommy had nothing to bet, since all his mining income went to support his family. So instead, they got him to take a dare. If he lost, he had to run stark naked back to his house."

Nikki Jo chuckles, then calls Mira Brooke to her side. She picks her up and snuggles with her as the story continues. I quietly fix a barbeque sandwich, pile on the coleslaw, and take my first blissful bite.

"Of course, being half-snockered, poor old Tommy-boy lost. But it was winter, you see. Snow piled everywhere as it often does. Our Tommy wasn't about to break his word, no siree Bob. He gathered up his clothes and shoes and ran, buck naked, back to his parents' house at the top of the hill."

We all know how the story ends, except Charlotte and Stella, and the two listeners are a study in contrasts. Charlotte bites her fingernail and leans in toward Roger, anxious to hear the ending. Stella absently twirls a piece of hair, eyes fixed on a tree.

"So about ten years later, they wanted to rename the town. Those troublemaker boys never let Tommy's mortifying story die, and they suggested "BuckNekkid." Of course it was a joke, but no one could come up with anything better. And guess who got voted the first mayor of BuckNekkid? Our own Thomas McBride. Over the years, the name sort of broke down to "Buckneck," which is a good sight more respectable. But if you go back in the town records, you'll see what a big role our family played in its founding."

Charlotte claps and Roger leans back in his chair, pleased. "How about some of that banana pudding, Nikki Jo? About time for dessert, I'd say."

Petey walks Mira Brooke out to the yard. The lightning bugs flit from the grass like sparkling embers. Mira Brooke dances in excitement, her chubby bare feet sinking deep in the natural green carpet. What a blessed, near-idyllic childhood my daughter will have, growing up surrounded by this loving family.

Thomas relaxes in the waning light and wraps my waist with his arm. He whispers in my ear. "Didn't have any idea you were marrying Buckneck royalty, did ya, Mrs. Spencer?"

I love my husband's warm, masculine smell. As I turn to him, he flashes me one of his huge smiles that make my stomach flip. I give him a quick, soft kiss on those perfect lips.

The deep murmur of Andrew's voice carries down the table as he's deep in conversation with Charlotte. Meanwhile, Stella has vanished. I give her the benefit of the doubt and assume she's helping Nikki Jo get the coffee and dessert dishes. I should be doing that myself, but I'm hypnotized by the heady, luxuriant lull of summer.

My cell phone buzzes in my pocket, breaking the spell. I extricate myself from the picnic bench and walk into the yard. "Yes?"

"Mrs. Spencer, it's Detective Tucker. Don't worry about getting hold of Tawny Creeden."

"Oh, you found her? Great! Did she call you?"

"I went over to the spa tonight to check on things and keep an eye on the woods. I'm afraid I got to her too late."

"Got to her? What do you mean? What happened?" Even as I ask, my intuition supplies the answer.

"She was killed today, by an arrow. Lowlife threw her in the excavation site...I don't have a lot of details, but it looks like she was dragged a ways. Forensics should be able to tell us more."

Nikki Jo emerges from the house, carrying her multi-layered banana pudding in a scalloped serving bowl. I feel like the top of my head is missing. I should have brought Tawny into the reception area, instead of having her wait in her car. I should have given her a little information so she could go back and write up a story. What if the killer locked us in the sauna so he could kill Tawny? What if she was screaming outside and we never heard her?

Detective Tucker's voice drones on, and I miss most of what he's saying, but I do catch "not your fault" and "I've called her husband."

Thomas' strong arms encircle me and I slump into them, dropping the phone into my pocket. I don't even know if I hung up.

Thomas murmurs, "What's going on, Tess?"

Nikki Jo rushes to my side. "Are you light-headed? Come on inside and sit in the study where it's nice and quiet."

After they walk me into the house, I drop to the couch and try to explain Tawny's death—something that is inexplicable on every level. I feel sick for ruining such a perfect family evening. Yet part of me itches to pick up my Glock, camp out in the spa parking lot, and blow that killer to kingdom come when he comes back around.

There seems to be no way to evade this invisible rogue hunter. To turn the tables, someone has to expose him before he can strike again.

17

The twisted root of Sea's jocular attitude toward me has been exposed. She has been plotting against me. Emmett, the master guide (leader) of our commune, approached me today. Apparently Sea told him some fib that I attacked her that day we sat and talked religion. I feel stabbed in the back, betrayed. I did nothing untoward, but now I almost wish I had to warrant this venom.

How did I react, you might wonder. First of all, I walked out on Emmett. I didn't confirm or deny the allegations against me. It is beneath me to even have to consider responding to something so inane.

I went back to my room, which I share with three other people, and packed what little I own. All I care about is saving enough to have a place of our own when you come to live with me. Please don't fret. I will find a cheap place to live in the interim and continue saving.

Even as I packed, Sea bounced in, all shining hair and eyes. It felt like a trap, like she wanted to get me alone. I ignored her attempts at conversation and will admit I wished the earth would open and swallow her up. Conniving ingrate.

I won't write to you until I'm settled somewhere. In the meantime, please be comforted knowing the universe will protect me, since I am one of its wisdom-bearers.

Late in the night, as the box fan thrums and Thomas and Mira Brooke sleep, I formulate a plan. Today will be official Train-to-Kill-a-Killer Day on the Spencer ranch. We can shoot our pistols out on the property and rehearse proper trunk escape procedure. I'll ask Charlotte over and Nikki Jo might join in, too. Maybe we can even serve refreshments. I want the women in my life ready if they run into this psycho. Stella will just have to operate from her own non-violent handicap, even though I'm fairly certain Andrew will participate.

Explaining the idea to Thomas takes less time than I expect, especially when I throw in the magic words: "Detective Tucker." After all, the man did tell me to carry my gun and find out how to get out of a trunk.

Thomas is less enthusiastic with the idea of closing me in his trunk, however. We watch several YouTube videos on escape techniques and I figure I'll be doing great if I can keep my wits about me in the tight space. Mira Brooke cavorts around the living room with her dollies while I discover how to kick rear brake lights out.

By afternoon, we have all assembled at the range, a dirt bunker out in one of Roger's fields. Nikki Jo finally agreed to join us, as long as we let her bring along lemonade and sandwiches. Nikki Jo's primary aversion to guns is that they mess with her manicures. Despite that, my blondie mother-in-law is a deadeye shooter, putting even Thomas and Andrew's skills to the test.

Charlotte hugs me when she arrives, her camo pants looking more vogue than utilitarian. "You okay?"

"I'm going to be. We're going to get ready for whatever comes next."

"I hope that doesn't include your returning to that spa, girl. Hey, where's my little peach today?"

"Stella agreed to keep Mira Brooke up at the big house. You know Andrew couldn't resist coming along for some bloodsport."

Charlotte gives a throaty laugh. "Those two don't seem...well-matched."

"Andrew and his girlfriends rarely do."

She nods. Thomas walks our way. The combination of the Smith & Wesson hitched in his belt holster, faded jeans, and masculine stubble add up to something irresistible. I give him a kiss.

"You two," Charlotte says, grinning. She walks over to chat with Nikki Jo, diverting Andrew from his gun preparations in the back of Roger's truck. Roger begins to set up targets with Petey.

We take turns shooting, youngest to oldest. Petey is also a crack shot, and he loves shooting Thomas' .45. Charlotte borrows my Glock, because she still doesn't have her own gun, much to everyone's chagrin.

"What if this killer stalks women?" Andrew asks her, his stubble beard grown out a day or two beyond Thomas'. He wears his beloved Birkenstocks and green surfer shorts, topped by an incongruous *Jurassic Park* T-shirt he might have had when he was a teen. He'd be hard to take seriously if that Spencer-dude air of aristocracy didn't cling to him. "I mean, what if he watches women? You're right there in the middle of town, in that big old house. Wouldn't be hard to break in. You know what I mean. You're *noticeable*. You need to be extra careful, Charlotte."

Roger, Thomas, and Petey all chime in with suggestions as to how Charlotte can watch her back. Nikki Jo starts setting up the ham and cheese sandwiches. She already out-shot all of us, hitting the bulls-eye nearly every time.

After a couple more rounds of shooting, we sit down to eat. Nikki Jo, Roger, and Petey return to the big house to get Mira Brooke down for her nap. Charlotte and I need to try our hand at trunk escape, and Thomas' 1980 Volvo fits the bill. No pop-up safety latches with that baby.

The fact we're going through with this is a testament to how safe we feel with these guys. Knowing my fear of small spaces, Charlotte volunteers to try it first. Thankfully, the Volvo has a spacious trunk, given her long legs. She folds into the cavernous black space and Thomas gently shuts the lid.

She's supposed to search for ways to get out and then bang on the lid twice when she feels like she's found them. After a few muffled thuds and metallic clinks, she pounds the lid and Thomas opens it. Andrew offers his hand, gallantly helping her climb out.

I give her a hug. "So? What was it like?" I need to know.

"First of all, it was brighter than I thought," she says. "Sunlight filtered in through the cracks and the brake lights. I think kicking into the light cavities would be no problem. But this all hinges on one thing: I would have to have my hands and feet free. Is that how they were, Tess?"

Everyone looks to me, and I don't even want to speculate. Mostly likely the women's legs and arms weren't bound, because they were probably dead before they were placed in the trunk. I don't want to go there in my mind. We're focusing on live-kidnap escape methods.

Andrew seems to sense the morbid reason for my silence. "Tess, what about this. We could tie you up and see if you can—"

"Not on your life," Thomas interrupts.

"Wait," I say. "This could happen, to me or to Charlotte or even to your mom. We need to be prepared. Duct tape my hands and feet."

Thomas looks sullen as a scolded child. I stick to my guns, determined to override his reticence. "Do it."

After a brief stand-off, Thomas reluctantly pulls the roll of tape from his tool kit. Charlotte looks desperate. "Let me go in there, Tess. You don't have to do this."

I think of Dani's spider story. There was more than a kernel of truth in it. To get past this claustrophobia, I need to make myself overcome it—to crush it. I have to keep a level head if the serial killer gets his hands on me. "This is actually one thing I *have* to do. Now stop coddling me and let's get on with it."

I put my arms behind my back. Thomas slowly wraps a strip around my wrists, then stops abruptly. "I can't."

Charlotte takes over, gingerly wrapping my wrists and ankles. As Thomas and Andrew hoist me into the trunk, Andrew jokes, "Good thing you're a lightweight shortie, Tess."

Thomas shoots him a death glare. Charlotte's warm amber gaze speaks louder than words, but she closes the trunk.

Blackness. No air. Only glimmers of light. No way out.

I force myself to breathe evenly, despite the sweat that quickly dampens my shirt. I face the trunk opening, hands behind me. The brake lights are slightly backlit by sunlight. I think I could kick out a light from this position. I tentatively push toward one with my boots. Sure enough, I could dislodge or break it and shove my feet out.

I stretch my arms back. Even with their limited range, I could grope around for items to use for weapons. If I twisted around, I could kick into the back seat. Anything to make driving difficult for the kidnapper, they say.

Things are looking hopeful, as long as I'm conscious when I go into the trunk. I could do this. I force myself to take a couple more deep, measured breaths, then kick the trunk twice.

It opens immediately, three shadows hovering just beyond. Thomas has his knife ready and cuts the duct tape, then hoists me out. He looks more apologetic than I've ever seen him. "I don't like seeing you like that...helpless, like when you were in labor with Mira

Brooke."

"It all turns out fine in the end." I smile. "I love you all. Thank you for being here while I did that. Now we're ready to roll."

18

So sorry it's been five months since I've written. Much has happened in that time, much I can't really explain. Suffice it to say, I'm still working at Woolworth's and I have a place to live. Just send your letters to this P.O. address.

I was sorry to hear of your mother's strange disappearance. Thank you for letting me know, although I'm not sure why you asked if I knew anything about it. I haven't contacted your mother for months and I certainly wouldn't seek her out willingly. It is odd that she left, given that she's not a real self-starter. I thought she'd stay in that house forever, nursing the hopes of reuniting with you and trying to forge a "family" of us again.

I've discovered I have a new skill: acting. Every time Julie reprimands me, I become penitent, groveling loudly like a jilted lover. It's appalling, but it's impressive how quickly it shuts her flapping mouth because it highlights what an oppressor she is. I did this one day when the store owner came to visit. I stayed late just to watch him haul Julie into the office to be reprimanded. I'm not above assisting karma so I watch it play out in this lifetime.

On Sunday the Spencer clan attends church. Stella deigns to make an appearance, astonishingly clad in a tube-top and fitted short skirt. Nikki Jo makes a point of putting as much distance as possible between herself and Stella on our pew.

Mira Brooke loves the nursery and nearly jumps out of my arms every time I drop her off. She's the kind of child who loves variation from routine and embraces new people. I lean on the top of the nursery's Dutch door, watching her glossy curls bob toward the toy box, her fluffy green dress cushioning her when she tumbles back into a sitting position. She grips the doll she's plundered and pulls herself up to investigate again. Intrepid little sweetie.

Last year was the first time I'd returned to church since I was a kid. Since then, I've attended two women's Bible studies with Nikki Jo and learned more than I ever thought I could. It's like my eyes are opened and nearly every time I read the Bible now, it speaks to me. Thomas is excited with my change of heart toward all things spiritual and I am too. I had pretty much written Jesus off after my childhood and college experiences, but as it turns out, Jesus never wrote me off.

After a huge meal at Nikki Jo's, Thomas and I bow out for naptime—Mira Brooke's and ours. There is something positively tranquilizing about Sundays after church.

But before we leave, the doorbell rings, launching Thor into a burst of manic barking. Roger, still wearing his blue striped oxford-cloth shirt, bow tie, and penny loafers, strides over to open the door. Low voices murmur, then Roger returns to the dining room.

"Detective Tucker is here to see you, Tess."

Nikki Jo cranes her neck, trying to get a glimpse of her childhood friend. Unable to see around the dining room wall, she gives up that tactic and plows ahead of me, hand outstretched, to the front door.

"Zeke! Fancy meeting you here! Law...I haven't seen you in a coon's age!"

Detective Tucker loses his usual commanding vibe. "Nikki Jo," he says. "You haven't changed a bit."

"Why, thank you. How's Tilly? And your children?"

"All fine, thank you kindly for asking."

Silence falls over the two of them. I feel like there's more back-story here, but it's none of my beeswax.

"Come on in for coffee and pie?" Nikki Jo offers.

"I'd love to, but I really need to get back. Just needed to talk with your girl here."

Once again, I love how I'm lumped right in with the Spencers as if I've been one of them all my life.

"Of course, sure thing. You tell Tilly I said hello." Nikki Jo pats my arm and returns to the dining room. Wild yelps ricochet from upstairs and I'm sure Petey's holding Thor back from making a mad dash outside. I walk out on the porch and sit in a rocker, unable to think what to say.

"It's not your fault." Detective Tucker reads my mind. "Mrs. Creeden was determined to get the scoop and who knows, she might have nosed around the wrong person. Reason I'm here is that she did work up a story for *The Buckneck Daily* and we found it on her computer. Guess who she'd been talking to that very day she disappeared? Mr. Byron Woods."

"What? What could he know? He was just a hanger-on, doing computer repairs at the spa."

"Apparently, he was watching and taking notes...meaning he stumbled onto the fresh body that morning and told Tawny about it. He was also particularly interested in why *you* didn't want him seeing the crime scene."

"Insinuating I was somehow involved? How dare he?"

"The article had some other interesting ideas, but it wasn't complete yet. For one thing, Mrs. Creeden was snooping around the truck stop bathroom. She thought she'd figured out how the killer took Melody Carroll— our motorcyclist victim."

Melody. Tawny. Was there something about the names the killer liked? Probably a long shot.

"Detective Tucker, do you have a list of names of all the victims?"

"Yes, happy to get that to you. Why?"

"Off the top of your head, do you know if their names all ended in 'y'?"

He shifts in his chair. "No. Not as I recall. So far the only connection is that three of the earliest victims were from California, so the killer might have lived there in the late eighties, when the first killing occurred. But how the bodies wound up across the country, I'd love to know. And outside those first three, the rest came from the Midwest, the South...all over the place. The only victim from West Virginia is Tawny Creeden, so I have to believe she somehow got too close."

I'm still ticked that both Tawny and Byron were

aware of the dead body that morning at the spa, but they acted oblivious about it. "Have you checked her computer history, like what she was Googling, that kind of thing?"

"No, but I'll get right on that and let you know. Like I told you earlier, our resources are stretched pretty thin."

A wild-eyed Thor bursts from the door, loosely attached to the leash in Petey's hand. The yipping dog makes a beeline for Detective Tucker's leg and starts sniffing as if preparing to use the bathroom.

Petey pulls at the leash. "Stop that! Sorry, Detective Tucker. He acted like he had to go."

Detective Tucker stands. "I won't take up any more of your fine Sunday, Mrs. Spencer. But you're going in to work tomorrow, correct?"

I haven't talked to Dani, but I figure I'm still on the roster. "I think so."

"Text me when you get there and when you leave. Just in case."

Just in case some killer gets to me before he can.

19

~*~

Things are escalating so rapidly at work, I decided to go back to the college and see if I could teach again. I gave the dean a spiel about how living at the commune helped me refocus, recharge, renovate...whatever words I felt he wanted to hear. Sadly, my acting routine didn't work on him and he told me in no uncertain terms that I was not welcome back on campus.

But we should talk about you. You are in a new home now. Do they treat you well? Do they have children your age? Do you ever tell them about me? I do hope every family you're with knows that your father loves you and will take you back when you turn sixteen. Not before then as I still need to save money and I want you old enough to enjoy traveling to West Virginia with me.

Did I tell you I recently went there? It was beautiful, though the snowy roads were treacherous. I was able to hunt a bit and pack up my own venison before I left. I am looking forward to taking you there next year so we can hunt together.

Dani steps out of her car when I arrive. She's carrying an ivory satchel purse in one hand and a green smoothie in the other. She says hi but her eyes travel to my belt. Is she looking for my gun?

"I'm carrying." I hope that's what she wanted to hear.

She nods. "You a pretty good shot?"

"I'm no Annie Oakley, but I can usually hit what I'm aiming at, yes. I practiced this weekend. What about you?"

She looks startled. "Me?"

"Well, I assume you shot guns as a Marine? They utilize weaponry there, do they not?"

"Oh, that. Yes, I did. That was so long ago. I've followed a more peaceful path since then."

I can't repress a smirk. "You did? I could swear that chokehold wasn't too peaceful."

She coughs. "Again—sorry about that. I thought it was the greater good in that situation. Hey, have you checked the computers to see if they're working now? I got the invoice from that guy. It's astronomical!"

"Yeah, I figured." I wish I could fill Dani in on Byron's kibitzing with a reporter. Which reminds me. "Did Detective Tucker tell you about Tawny Creeden?"

"Yes. Good gracious. That poor woman. I mean, she wasn't my favorite person, nosing around like that. I only wish Detective Tucker would tell me how they're being killed. It should probably be in the paper that there's a serial killer out there, don't you think? So we know how to protect ourselves?"

I keep forgetting Detective Tucker hasn't told Dani that this killer is a bowhunter. He needs to. There's no reason I can see to keep it under wraps, but he'll have to be the one to tell her.

"I agree. Women need to be prepared."

As we fall into our routines, I text Detective Tucker to let him know I'm at the spa. He texts back that he's in his office today, compiling records on the dead women.

Teeny arrives, his thinning hair more askew than usual. "Howdy. Dani here?"

"She's in the back, checking the chlorine in the pool. Though we won't have any swimmers today, I imagine. You have some massages lined up?"

"I do. Here's the list of names." He pulls a crumpled yellow paper from his pants pocket, which looks like it's been splattered with pop and smeared with the artificial orange of a cheese puff.

"Thanks." I play a hunch. "Say, Teeny, you ever

go hunting? My husband likes to hunt."

"Sure. Grew up hunting."

"Bow or rifle?"

"I used to bowhunt a lot, but don't have a good tree stand now I'm living at Momma's. I have to go to my cousin's to hunt. He bugs me and then we get into fights. So I don't hunt anymore."

"Oh, okay. My husband uses a rifle."

The door swings open and Axel walks in, carrying a jaw-dropping bouquet of sunflowers, dahlias, and full pink roses. Teeny gapes as Axel carries it over to my desk. I feel like a shrimp in the middle of the *Clash of the Titans*. Teeny is wider than Axel, but Axel is a hair taller. I don't know why I tend to picture Axel in fight situations, but I do.

"What's this?" I ask as Teeny continues to size up the German giant.

"It is an apology bouquet for your owner because I entered without permission. Courtesy of Fabled Flowers. Should she want flowers provided on a regular basis, she can call our shop for details."

That's how to win friends and influence people, right there. I touch the lavish, vibrant blooms, wondering if we have a vase in the back. I'm guessing Axel also dropped by to scope out the situation at the spa today.

He turns to Teeny. "You are an employee?"

Teeny looks affronted. "Yeah, I work here."

Neither says a word. Axel's powerful jaw flexes. Teeny sniffs. I stand to get a vase.

Teeny breaks first. "I'll get on back there." He trudges toward his massage room.

Axel gives me a look. I shrug, reading his thoughts. I don't know if Teeny locked us in the sauna, but it's a possibility.

Abruptly, Axel strides out the front door. I watch him get in his car, then I head for the kitchen. Raiding the cabinets, I finally turn up a coffee mug stout enough to support the bouquet's sturdy stems.

Once I situate both the flowers and myself at the front desk, I check out the computer. It seems to run fine, but it did that before. What if Byron installed some kind of hacking tracker? We'd never know.

Dani comes out, her sleeves slightly wet from messing with the pool. "I have a henna job and two aromatherapy facials scheduled for this afternoon. I'll plug the names into the computer now."

She notices the bouquet. "Let me guess. From that German florist."

"Yes. He wanted to apologize for coming into your spa and he wanted to show you a sample of his flowers."

"I must say I'm more impressed than I thought I would be. This caliber bouquet could hold its own in a Manhattan spa. Is he taken?"

I glance at her, thinking she's joking. But the

hopeful glint in her level gaze tells me she's serious. I can't really picture the two of them together, but what do I know?

"I don't think so. Did you...want me to give him your number or something?"

"I'll contact him sometime. Actually, once this killer is caught, I was thinking of having a fancy reception at the spa. Celebrate the return of the hairstylists, all that. He could do the flowers for it."

"Great idea." I don't give voice to my thoughts. If the killer isn't caught soon, the Crystal Mountain Spa will be relegated to one of those West Virginia ghost-hunter lists. Dani will have to kiss her business goodbye.

When Charlotte arrives, bearing homemade split pea soup and bread for me, I recognize the poorly-hidden look of despair on her face. She's been cooking up a storm to escape The Haven.

"Miranda okay?" I ask.

Her smile wavers and crumples. "She's not good. Caught some kind of bug and the coughing wracks her entire body."

I picture Miranda, sitting like a queen, white hair perfectly coiffed, hosting a catered dinner at her dining room table for Paul Campbell and me. How could that have been less than two years ago?

"I'll come visit her tomorrow, okay?"

"Sounds good." She sniffs the roses. "Gorgeous. I have a delicate pink vase I glazed that these would look great in."

"Feel free to bring it by for display and throw in some of your business cards too, potter-girl. The flowers are from Axel."

"How do I always miss seeing him? He's very mysterious."

"Ain't that the truth? This soup is making my mouth water. Want to eat outside?"

As we knock stray leaves off the patio table, it dawns on me that we can't eat out here, so close to the ferny woods. We're easy targets if a crazed bowhunter wants to take a shot from some hidden lair.

I pick up the thermos of soup. "We actually need to eat inside. I forgot."

Charlotte's gaze follows mine to the woods. "Oh, right. Killer on the loose and all that. No problem."

In a flash of déjà vu, Teeny comes out, looking like he plans to join us. Thankfully, Dani is close behind him, toting her earth-friendly paper bag lunch. "Lunchtime? Hi, Charlotte."

"We were going back inside to be safe," I say.

Teeny maneuvers his large frame into a smaller chair, balancing a smelly burrito on a paper towel on his knee. "No one will kill us when we're all out here."

I'm not so confident about safety in numbers with a bowhunter, but I might get some information from this captive audience. Sadly, all I know about the killer is a big fat "not much." The fact that those first victims were from California niggles at me, because I know Dani used to live there. But the first victim was in the 1980s and she would have been young.

"Teeny and I were talking about hunting this morning," I say.

Charlotte tilts her face toward me, recognizing my probing tone.

"Did you ever go hunting, Dani? Back in your Marine days, I mean."

Teeny jerks his head up, half-chewed burrito in his gaping mouth. "You were a Marine?"

Dani crosses her legs, her ivory suede heels creating a lean line with her pale blue pants. "As I said, those times are behind me."

I smile. "Sorry. Just trying to get to know each other. I'm an only child and so is Charlotte. What about you all?"

"Me too," Teeny says around a mouthful. Charlotte turns her head, unwilling to face the grossness.

"I have a couple sisters," Dani says. "They're in Oregon."

The patio door opens and we all jump, since we're

not expecting any clients. Byron walks out in all his mismatched, nerd-chic glory. Charlotte arches an eyebrow. I'm not sure if she's thinking *This guy is hot* or *Pull your gun now, Tess.*

He runs his eyes appreciatively over all the women and ignores Teeny. "I'm looking for Danielle Gibson?"

Dani stands. "Yes?"

My hand drops to the Glock.

He strides toward her. "Just came to settle the score."

20

I've been lonely, almost missing the bustle and racket of the commune. Or perhaps I miss you. I know it's not your mother I'm missing. Although I am sorry no one has heard from her.

I went on a date with a woman from work. I'm embracing my freedom, but it only seemed to make me feel more hollow. Today's women are so forward. Even as she plastered her sticky bright peach lips on my cheek, I pushed her away. I am not looking for that; it insults my intelligence. I believe I'm pining for conversation, such as the one I had with Sea. In those precious moments, she looked to me as the teacher I am. I don't know why she turned on me with such heartlessness, but who knows, maybe she was stoned at the time she made the accusation.

I should probably follow up with her and get to the bottom of her false complaint. Perhaps I will.

Teeny jumps up, dropping the remainder of his burrito. He moves in front of Dani, glaring murderously at Byron. "What do you want?"

Byron looks confused. "Just like I said—settling up debt. I need payment on your computer repair job so I can get a new hard drive for my laptop. It's on sale this week."

Dani pats Teeny's shoulder. He slowly walks back to his chair, leaving the offensive burrito in a splat on the patio tile. As Dani leads Byron inside, I try to figure out why she would agree to pay him on such short notice.

Charlotte stands and stretches, ignoring Teeny's appreciative stare. I know she's relieved things didn't deteriorate into a shootout at the Crystal Mountain Spa. "I gotta run, Tess. Stop in tomorrow to see Mom, okay? Maybe around four?"

She whisks past Teeny. He sighs as she closes the door. "Could you give me her phone number?"

I laugh. "Not a chance."

As the afternoon slowly ticks by, I'm haunted by

images of Melody and Tawny. I can picture them alive and healthy at the spa, and I can just as easily picture them bleeding to death with an arrow through the heart. I wish I knew what I was looking for, what kind of behavior would give this hunter away. I've watched several Lifetime movies about serial killers, but that hardly makes me an expert.

Teeny leaves around three, and Dani starts closing up at four. We walk together to the parking lot.

"See you tomorrow, Tess. That was weird that Byron came by, but I paid him off since he was so anxious to buy a new hard drive. I can tell our computers are running better."

"I'm glad you think so." I don't voice my opinion that they've hardly changed. "See you later."

With her usual flourish, Dani guns it down the drive. I text Detective Tucker that I'm leaving, then roll down my window to air out the car before I turn on the air conditioning.

A flash of white glints in the woods. I look closer, but can't make out what it is. Then I hear a faint engine rev and it moves deeper into the trees. It's a vehicle of some kind. Could that be Byron's van?

I pray first, then quietly leave the safety of my SUV. As I walk toward the woods, I pull my Glock. Plunging into the ferny green cover, I quickly spot the wider path. The woods are like a second skin to me, a place I slip into comfortably like a baby moving in the womb. It shouldn't be hard for me to hide and stalk this vehicle.

The tire tracks are still evident and I follow them for about twenty minutes, but the vehicle got a head start and I can barely catch a glimpse of it. I finally come to a break in the treeline, where I see the truck stop in the distance. There are no cars in sight.

My gut feeling tells me that Melody was killed somewhere between the truck stop and the Crystal Mountain Spa. Possibly Tawny was killed in this area too.

I hike back into the woods, watching for any signs of movement. The day has turned hot and muggy, pushing ninety degrees. I'm thankful Mira Brooke can spend the days up at Roger and Nikki Jo's, in their air-conditioned house. We only have fans in our cottage, but on days like this when the air is dead, it gets oppressive fast.

Even the leaf-carpeted forest floor seems to emanate heat beneath me, scalding under the unrelenting gaze of the sun. The welcome rustle of running creek water wafts my way. I turn into the brush to check it out, keeping my eyes open for anything unusual.

It's a good-sized creek, with a few tiny minnows dancing just under the surface. There's a deep green area that was probably used as a swimming hole years ago. I wonder who owns this land? I could probably ask Thomas.

I'm looking for anything out of place, anything *human* in this natural landscape. But nothing catches my eye...until something catches my nose.

The stench of rotting flesh bulldozes my senses. I point the Glock and follow the smell, hoping it doesn't belong to a victim. Just over a rocky incline, I see the source and exhale. Just a dead deer. But as I get closer, I realize it's not some random deer. This deer has been gutted for venison...and it's not hunting season. Someone's poaching in these woods.

Either there are a lot of lawbreakers around, or this poacher is one and the same as the killer. It seems like someone needs to keep a close eye on this forest, but that's not my job. I'll call Detective Tucker when I get back.

Something catches my eye—an abnormal structure under a swath of ferns. I move closer and pull the green tendrils aside. Two thin, short logs are tied together with twine to form a rough cross. The anchor log is firmly lodged in the ground. Someone deliberately placed this here, maybe years ago. A gravestone? A memorial? A whim? Rock slabs jut from the ground in this area, so it's not the most effective burial spot. But I make a note of the location to tell Detective Tucker.

The woods seem empty today, devoid of anything living except me. I know this is an illusion, that animals are camped out where I can't see them. I'm quite sure no humans are hiding here, or I'd sense it. The heavy silence comforts me as I make my way back, relaxing my hold on the gun.

But as the spa comes into view, I tighten my grip, pulling the Glock closer with both hands. Detective Tucker's Hummer sits parked next to my SUV, and he lounges against it. At least he gives the appearance of lounging. As I get closer, I see he's holding his archaic cell phone in one hand and a large .45 in the other. He's not messing around.

"Mrs. Spencer. I've been trying to get a hold of you. Where were you? Your car's sitting here and you're not in the spa—"

"I'm sorry, the wireless signal was out of range. I followed a car that was in the woods...I thought it might be Byron." I try to channel a look of childlike innocence.

His eyes flash. He's obviously not affected by my spiel. "The woods? I want you to stay out of there. I'm keeping an eye on it. And I plan to check into Byron's history as soon as I can." He pockets his cell phone and sheathes his gun, but the tension doesn't leave his voice. "Mrs. Spencer, I came here to tell you something. You might want to sit down."

Nothing good has ever followed those words. I open my SUV door and sit in the driver's seat. "Okay, I'm ready."

"Your friend, Charlotte Michaels, went missing

outside The Haven today. The receptionist saw her leave, but her car is still parked in the lot."

A guttural scream works its way up my throat. Starting as a growl, it ends in a fierce battle cry I can't repress. Detective Tucker doesn't step closer, doesn't try to intervene or comfort me.

"He's getting careless," he says, when I finally lapse into silence. "Like I said, I'm going to stake out the spa and woods tonight. But I want you back at home, Mrs. Spencer."

I'm not going to my home. I will stay at Charlotte's house in town until she returns. Because she will come back. She has to.

21

~*~

Would you believe I ran into Sea at the grocery store? I couldn't believe my luck. I told her we needed to talk. She agreed, albeit with a toss of her thick brown hair. After setting up a place and time, I left, feeling lighter in my spirit. This was good; this was closure. I was pursuing truth, which is a noble thing.

Julie went into a fit of histrionics the other day, shouting about my perceived ineptitudes on the job. I took it like a man. After work, I waited up and stopped her before she got to her car. I wanted to reason with her, one-on-one. I asked her why she had such a bee in her bonnet about me and she couldn't articulate it properly, harpy that she is. I would like to say I remained non-violent, but my temper did rise from the abyss and get the better of me.

We are closing in on your last year in foster care. Are you excited? I hope you have been preparing yourself for our hunting adventures. We will truly make an unstoppable team.

When I explain to Thomas and Nikki Jo, they understand my need to stay at Charlotte's tonight. I stop by our house to love on Mira Brooke, who will stay up at the big house with her grandparents. Thomas is getting home late from work anyway.

I have the key to Charlotte's green house. After parking in her spot on the curb, I walk up the porch steps and realize Andrew was right when he said the old house would be easy enough to break into. The windows are old and easily jiggered, the basement door hangs limply on its hinges, and the street is poorly lit. It's a perfect storm of vulnerability.

Gripping my duffel bag, I unlock the door and feel along the wall for a light switch. As in many old houses, the switch is in a strange place, and you have to push it, like a button on an elevator. When the living room lights up, I step all the way inside. My Glock sits snug on my waist and I swiped Thomas' hunting knife, for good measure. I hooked the knife sheath on my belt. If I had one more pistol and wore boots and shorts, I'd feel even more like Tomb Raider.

Charlotte spent a lot of time cleaning and

decorating the house, and the entire place seems to breathe her name. Miranda's antiques are juxtaposed with splashy modern artwork on the walls. Unique ceramics crowd every flat surface. I love Charlotte's large, jellybean-shaped bowls that look like art but serve up popcorn equally well.

Her kitchen is in a disarray, as if she whisked out quickly this morning. The dry-erase board on her fridge holds no clues as to her whereabouts; it just says *fish, linguine,* and *eggs.*

I know full well Charlotte wouldn't have waltzed off with someone without telling me. She was planning to see her mom and then go home. She would have no reason for leaving her car at The Haven parking lot. It's too far to walk to her house from there. Something happened to her...*someone* happened. I walk back into the living room and drop into a celery-colored Queen Anne chair. Tears flow fast and unregulated.

Our hands are helplessly tied. Sure, the police are trying to track any clues, follow up with any witnesses who saw her leave. But the thing is, this stalker strikes fast and deadly. The one thing that comforts me is that he probably wouldn't risk shooting her with a bow in the parking lot, and they've found no blood. He is probably taking her to his lair, wherever that is. But how does he shoot the women once he has them? Does he drug them first, then shoot them? And why am I calling this killer a "he?" It could just as easily be a woman.

I move to the black leather couch, set my Glock on the floor, and pull a faded garden-patterned quilt over myself. I can't eat, even though I'm fairly certain Charlotte has a well-stocked fridge and would want me to. She would tell me to take care of myself. But she's the one who needs someone looking out for her now. I pray out loud, begging God to spare her life. Even as I pray, I start drifting off to sleep.

My cell phone rings around 1:15 in the morning. Detective Tucker is on the other end.

"She's alive. Meet me at the Pleasant Valley Hospital. I'll be in the waiting room by the front door."

Dazed but praising God, I slip into my sandals, put my Glock back in its holster, and lock the house. I ease the SUV into the street with my park lights on, trying not to wake the neighbors.

I think of that verse I read yesterday about how beautiful upon the mountains are the feet of him who brings good news. Now I can understand a bit better what Isaiah was saying. There are times when the evil seems so impenetrable, the wickedness so victorious, you don't even know how to hope. But then the good news bursts in, as impossible to deny as it is to believe. *She's alive.*

I run into Bartholomew Cole in the parking lot as he rushes toward the hospital. The Good Doctor isn't looking his usual dapper self, because he's wearing a striped pajama shirt over khaki cargo shorts and his thick white hair is positively rumpled.

"Tess." He gives me a brief hug and takes my arm as we walk into the waiting room.

Detective Tucker hastens to my side, his dark eyes intense. "You two know each other?"

"Yes, this is Doctor Bartholomew Cole. He's dating Charlotte."

"I see. And where were you tonight, Doctor Cole?"

The Good Doctor looks surprised, realizing he's being questioned, but quickly regains his composure. "I just got in tonight from a conference in Missouri. Melva at the switchboard called to let me know they'd brought Charlotte in. What's going on?"

"Don't explain everything," I beg the detective. "Just tell us how she is."

"She's stable but out of it for now, since she lost a lot of blood from a heavy blow to the head," he says. "She somehow managed to show up at a house on the outskirts of Buckneck, pounding on the door around midnight. The homeowners called the police and we found her there, slumped in a heap by that point."

"Who would have done that? I don't understand." The Good Doctor looks at me incredulously, like he can't assimilate what the detective said.

I pat his hand. "I'll explain later, but I need to see her now."

Detective Tucker takes us both back, murmuring something to the police officer stationed by her door. I'm glad they had the decency to post someone here.

"No one comes in but me or the nurses and doctors, that's what I've told them," he explains.

Charlotte's deep brown hair forms a fuzzy halo around the bandages that wrap her head. Her angular cheekbones are pale, and they jut out more because her lips aren't quirked in her usual smile. I bend to kiss her, wiping away my silent tears that sprinkle her cheek. "Oh, Charlotte," is all I can say, over and over.

The Good Doctor takes her hand and checks her pulse. "They did a transfusion?" he asks. "Stitches or staples?"

"Several staples," Detective Tucker answers, almost apologetic. "It was Doctor Vasa. They tell me he's the best."

"Yes, he is. I'll have him paged so we can chat." The Good Doctor turns to me. "You can go home. I'll stay with her tonight and call you when she's awake. We're all lucky she got here in time." His gray eyes probe mine, earnest. "Tess, she's going to be okay."

The Good Doctor's spicy scent and insightful manner never fail to affect me. It's no wonder Charlotte fell for him. Sudden exhaustion claims me. "Okay, I'll head back to my house for now. Thank you."

Detective Tucker walks me out to the hallway. "Very sorry about your friend, Mrs. Spencer. But that's all the more reason for you to stay out of that woods. In fact, I'm going to advise Ms. Gibson to temporarily shut down the spa. I don't want you going back over there. I say this as a husband and a father. You don't need to risk your life for this case."

He's advising me to give up, but I know he's taking the same risks by staking out the woods. I want to share what I've found with the detective, but I can't think straight enough to sort it out at this hour. One fact leaps to mind, though.

"There's a poached deer carcass off the path, in the woods," I say. "And some kind of cross marker made from logs."

He rubs his beard. "That is unusual."

Thoughts rush at me and I try to articulate them, wishing for hot coffee to give my brain a needed jolt. "Also, Teeny told me he bowhunts."

"Good work."

I rub my bleary eyes. I need to get home while I'm half-lucid.

"Do you need a ride home, Mrs. Spencer? I can have one of my men take you."

"No, I'm okay. I just need to get going. Thank you and I'll call you tomorrow."

I walk out, my thoughts stationary, like snow

trapped under a crust of ice. I fumble with the SUV keys in the ignition. Once I'm on the road, I wake up a bit. One thing about the mountains: they're never boring. It's hard to drift to sleep when you're anticipating the direction of the next curve. They're a constant surprise, from ice fog that coats trees in winter to rockslides and deer any other time of year.

When I make the turn down our driveway, which always makes me feel like I'm taking a *Dukes of Hazzard*-style jump into space, I notice the porch light at the big house is on. Nikki Jo and Roger probably figured I could come back tonight and left it on for me. That little gesture melts me and tears flood my cheeks. I'm an emotional train wreck.

I finally crawl into bed beside Thomas around 4 a.m. His long arm wraps around my waist, pulling me into the curve of his body. He mumbles incoherently. "What, Tess...you love me?"

Even when he's rambling in his sleep, he's thinking about me. My hand covers his, and I fall asleep with his comforting pulse twitching under my thumb.

22

I have a bit of bad news. I'm afraid I'm no longer working at Woolworth's. I've also had to leave my apartment for now. There was an incident at work. I accidentally sliced Julie's ear with scissors. It was an honest mistake, I assure you. But she threatened to sue and management cut me loose as fast as possible. I will send you a new address when I have one, but it might be a while. I also have to job-hunt, this time with no references

Have you heard from your mother? I hope so. Then again, best not to suspend your own life, waiting for her. I am afraid she might have "flaked out," to use jargon you might be familiar with.

Continue the path to enlightenment. Read and work hard and develop your skills. Deepen your understanding of the universe. I will contact you as soon as possible.

Mira Brooke wakes me with her laughter as she kicks the side of her crib. Sunlight floods the room. How late have I slept? I grab my phone. It's 10:13.

I also have a text message from Nikki Jo. She's recently taken up texting, and reading her auto-corrected messages is invariably a hoot:

Honey I heard about charlatan and I am so sorry. I heard she is in the hospital. You need me to watch baby girl? Are you working at sap today? I have some chocolate Bambi muffins if you like.

I snicker when I read about her chocolate "Bambi" muffins, which should have read "banana" and are notoriously mouth-watering. I text her back.

Slept late. Staying home today with Mira Brooke. Will come up in a while and get some muffins though. Thanks. Love you.

I pull Mira Brooke out and kiss her rosy cheeks. As I change her diaper and clothes, I'm awed with my baby's happy demeanor, even after staying in her crib a couple hours past her normal wake-up time. Velvet wanders upstairs, meowing loudly for food and weaving between my legs. The cat is more demanding than the child.

I throw on my dark slim jeans and my favorite black *X-Files* T-shirt that reads *Trust No One*. Pretty much sums up why I'm not going in to work today.

As I walk Mira Brooke up to the big house, I take in our tranquil surroundings. The pale morning sun filters through the forest canopy around us. I imagine my dewy rosebush soaking it up, photosynthesizing like crazy. The coo of a mourning dove echoes, somehow soothing my heart. Sometimes I feel so entangled with the West Virginia seasons, it's like I'm breathing through them.

I smile, knowing Nikki Jo will have a fresh pot of coffee ready and my favorite creamer set out. She'll want to talk about Charlotte, which is exactly what I need to do right now to process things.

Nikki Jo meets me at her door, wearing sports garb since she hits her exercise equipment early. Today's ensemble includes electric yellow, green, and blue marbled leggings topped by a ruched green workout shirt. That outfit would be laughable on me, but Nikki Jo always looks like a knockout in bright colors.

As I give her the rundown on Charlotte over coffee and a muffin, she interjects numerous sighs and moans. "Bless that poor girl's heart," she says. "As if having her momma sick and nearly on her death-bed isn't enough. What's Zeke doing about this?"

"I guess we're all just waiting until Charlotte can tell us what happened. We need to ask if she saw who hit her, that kind of thing." I take a slow sip of coffee before plunging in with a question that's been burning in my mind. "Mom...tell me—were you and Zeke an item once?"

Her velvety brown eyes mist up. "Law, no. But he had a big crush on me. He wasn't as handsome then...he was what you'd call a nerd. But by my senior year I only had eyes for Roger. Roger was quarterback of the football team and he had that honey blond hair. I swan, he could just *look* at the girls and they'd drop like flies. I couldn't believe he fell for me." She smiles, lost in a different time and place.

I take another bite of muffin, waiting. Nikki Jo continues. "But I knew Zeke would make something of himself. He wasn't the kind of boy to sit idle. He had smarts and he was tough in ways most of the boys weren't. Put it this way—if some kind of catastrophe happened, he'd be the one I'd want around."

Mira Brooke babbles to herself, chocolate and muffin smeared all over her cheeks. "Petey!" Nikki Jo calls, wiping Mira Brooke's face. "Could you take Mira Brooke in with the toys for a while?"

Petey zooms into the kitchen, sliding across the floor in his sock feet. "Sure, Ma. Wanna play with your favorite uncle, Mir bear?" As soon as she's loose from her chair, Mira Brooke toddles off at top speed toward her play area.

Nikki Jo brings the coffee pot over, pouring us both a warm-up. "I know you have your gun, but I don't think you're safe at that spa. You don't need the income, do you? Especially when Thomas becomes the new prosecutor?"

My mother-in-law always encourages me to stay home with my daughter, and if I'm honest, part of me wants to just up and quit working. But we're still paying off law school debt, and Dani pays me well for the limited hours I put in. It's actually an ideal job, most of the time.

"I really do need the money, Mom. I'll talk with Dani. I told Detective Tucker I'd get the inside scoop, but so far I haven't learned much and he told me to quit going over, anyway. Maybe after this all blows over..."

"It's hard to catch a killer no one knows anything about." Nikki Jo levels a serious look at me over her red Fiesta-ware mug. She's fishing for details. If I share them, I'm sure everyone in Buckneck will know the killer's M.O. by noon. But maybe the Buckneck women *should* be aware of it. Why isn't Detective Tucker making it open knowledge the killer is a bowhunter? Maybe he's afraid people will start spying on their neighbors...but that might help us catch this murderer faster.

"I'll tell you as soon as I can." My cell phone starts

playing *Buffy*.

Nikki Jo plugs her ears with her fingers. "What on this green earth is that racket?"

"Sorry, Mom." I snatch it up. "Yes, Dani?"

"Where are you, Tess? I'm here at the spa by myself."

"I know. I couldn't come in. Charlotte's in the hospital. They're pretty sure the serial killer grabbed her."

"What? Why didn't anyone tell me? I'm always out of the loop and I should be the first to know any news. Tess, tell me. How is this stalker killing women? What kind of women? I have to know more. I'm sitting here *by myself*. Teeny didn't even show up, the slacker."

I won't be responsible for another friend becoming a victim. "It's a bowhunter. He's killing them with arrows."

Silence reigns on Dani's end. I look up, catching the stunned look on Nikki Jo's face. I could swear her to secrecy, but at this point I don't even care. The women of Buckneck need a fighting chance, and to be forewarned is to be forearmed—if there is any way to prepare for a mad bowhunter.

"Dani? You okay? Everything okay up there? You want me to cancel appointments from here? You should get home."

"Yes, I'm going to go. I'm locking up now, while we're talking. Hang on until I get to my car."

"Of course."

"Who would do this? Why?"

"Your guess is as good as mine. Serial killers aren't always predictable, I guess."

A car lock beep sounds, then her car door closes with a solid *wham*. Dani puts it on speaker phone and revs her engine. That girl loves to speed. She shouts into the car. "I'm okay and I'm out of here. Thanks for telling me."

"No problem. Let's just stay home until they catch him."

"It's a man? Are you sure?"

"No. I'm not sure of anything."

"Okay, well call me with news and tell Detective Tucker I expect the same courtesy from him. And Tess, I'm sorry about Charlotte. Is she okay?"

"I don't know, but I'm going to check today."

I hang up. Nikki Jo washes dishes in her deep farmhouse sink. She turns, accidentally swiping bubbles into her bangs.

"One of the best bowhunters I've ever known is Zeke Tucker." Doubt and fear have erased her usual dimples.

"It's not Detective Tucker." I try to project more confidence than I feel. *Trust No One* seems like the best way to proceed these days.

23

I sit here writing in the library, shocked that so many months have passed. I'm also shocked that it's your birthday month, and I am saddened at what I have to tell you.

I know for all these years, you must have looked forward to seeing me again, to living with me and learning from me. And believe me, I have anticipated that too, as you can tell from the volume of letters I have sent you in foster care.

A problem has arisen, one that can't be easily sidestepped. I need to go underground, so to speak. I can't have contact with you because they are watching for me to make a move.

I have so many words of wisdom to share with you. I have learned some lessons from the universe, and they have been hard to stomach. Something I have had to admit to myself, yet again, is that I am not meant to be a father.

Much as I dreamed of shaping you and sharing with you, my own childhood memories haunt me and render me incapable of deep love. My parents were far from ideal, and I am afraid I'll pass that heritage of poison on to you, even if I try to fight it. I had repressed many of the things they had said to me, but the dam of my memory has finally broken, and it can never be repaired.

I called your new foster mother and she said you're still searching for your mother. You need to stop wasting your time, chasing after the wind. She also said you've been acting out in school and have had too many absences. I cannot express my disappointment upon hearing that. You must keep up with your education and make plans to further it. I know I have no right to ask this of you, but in the end, I am your father.

I can't think what I need to write, but I know this must be my last letter to you. My thoughts have been scattered lately. Perhaps I will empty myself of my own knowledge, and instead leave you with a quote by someone else. I hope this will comfort you. Please understand, this distance we must maintain is for the best.

Here is a Rumi quote that is special to me: "Don't grieve. Anything you lose comes round in another form." I find that comforting, because no mistakes you make, no losses you suffer, are permanently damaging. Everything old will be new again and we will all get along. You will go far, my child, if you remember what I have taught you and dedicate yourself to excellence and wisdom. Do not let anyone stand in your way.

Nikki Jo and Petey keep Mira Brooke so I can check on Miranda and Charlotte. I'll visit Miranda first, because I know that's what Charlotte would want.

I'm surprised to see one of Thomas' police officer friends hanging out in the lobby at The Haven. He nods at me and I walk over to him.

"What's up?" I ask, trying to look casual.

"They have a resident who keeps leaving the building. Most of these people have freedom to come and go as they want, but some are restricted to staying on the premises for one reason or another, like if they don't have a license or if they have Alzheimer's. Probably that's the case with this one. We found him wandering outside town and brought him in this morning. How are you doing, Mrs. S?"

"Just fine, thanks. I was hoping nothing was wrong with my friend down in Suite 8A—Miranda Michaels."

"Nothing to do with her." He smiles and motions

me through. "You have a good one."

"You too."

I trudge down the hallway. I don't really want to know if Miranda is doing worse today. I don't want to consider the possibility she could die while Charlotte is in the hospital.

The nurse opens when I knock. "She's resting good today. Hasn't been talking much the past few days, though. You hear from her daughter lately?"

I explain how Charlotte is in the hospital, then I tiptoe in to see Miranda. Besides looking even more wizened than the last time I saw her, her breathing is regular and she seems stable. I silently sink to the floor by her bed, unable to stop thinking about the serial killer.

We just don't have enough to go on. The murderer could be anyone, male or female, young or old. So Teeny is a bowhunter? So is half the town. So Byron was talking with Tawny? It doesn't seem like he told her anything relevant. So Dani was in the Marines? Who cares. I just don't know what we're looking for, what the common denominator is.

Miranda murmurs in her sleep and I pat her hand. The nurse peeps in and motions to me. When I meet her in the living room, she waves her hands, talking rapidly. "I just thought of this, but one of the residents here seems overly fascinated with Charlotte. I'm wondering if he had anything to do with her attack."

"Define *overly fascinated*," I say.

"Every time she goes down to get food for her momma, he kind of trails behind her. And last time when she came in the suite, I caught him watching her out a crack in his door. He lives on this hall."

"Who is he?"

"Mr. Seger, they call him. He's right young compared to the others here. But he's more than a few pickles short of a jar, I'd say."

Mr. Seger. The man who accosted me in the hall here and the parking lot. I'm betting he's also the one the cops had to round up this morning.

"Thank you. I'm going to go now and check on Charlotte."

She gives me a pensive nod, then wanders into the kitchenette.

I walk in for one last moment with Miranda. I don't want to wake her, but I drop a light kiss on her hair. "Love you," I say. "And Mira Brooke is growing like a weed." I can't even say the word *Charlotte* without choking up, so I don't even go there.

When I get into my SUV, I text Detective Tucker.

Some dude here at The Haven has been stalking Charlotte. Plus he keeps escaping and he might be a little kooky. You might want to check on him: Mr. Seger. Don't know the first name. I'm not going in to the spa today and Dani left early. I told her about the

*arrows because I thought she needed to know. She
wants you to call her the minute you have any news.*

Next, I call Bartholomew Cole. The Good Doctor
should have gotten back to me by now, whether or not
there was any change with Charlotte. He picks up on
the third ring.

"Hello, Tess. Sorry I haven't called. It's been a
little touch-and-go with Charlotte. They woke her up
and she was disoriented and weak, so they wound up
transfusing more blood. She's stable but still not alert."

We chat a little more, then I drive to the hospital,
stopping by the new Chick-fil-A for a sandwich and a
large sweet tea. I can't resist a fresh-brewed, sugar-
sweet tea in the heat of summer.

In the hospital's gift shop, it takes a full five
minutes for the volunteer to ring up my bouquet choice,
which consists primarily of baby's breath. Its three
wilting pink roses look like they were thrown in as an
afterthought. Pink isn't Charlotte's favorite color, but
it's the best I can do right now. Next visit I'll bring
some of my own roses...but hopefully my next visit
will be to her home, not to the hospital.

In Charlotte's room, a tall, flawless bouquet of full
orange roses dominates the over-the-bed table,
blocking my view of her. I feel like chucking my sorry
excuse for a bouquet in the trash. The Good Doctor,
lounging in a chair by her bed, follows my gaze.

"I wish I could claim those. The card just says *Get Well Soon. From a Friend of Tess Spencer.*"

I open my mouth, about to protest any knowledge of the gift.

The doctor smiles. "Don't worry, Detective Tucker checked them out. They're from a legitimate florist in Point Pleasant—"

"Fabled Flowers," I finish.

"How'd you know?"

"I know the owner. What an extravagant...why did he do that?" I sniff the blooms, surprised to find they're fragrant, unlike most florist shop roses.

"He must be a good friend, I suppose? Or perhaps just an admirer." The Good Doctor winks at me. He's always hinting at what he perceives as my Buckneck bombshell status.

"Maybe." I let my gaze rest on Charlotte's face, blanched under its usual tan. "Still sleeping?"

"Yes, but she's more restless so I'm taking that as a good sign. She really does have some skilled doctors here."

After propping my tipsy bouquet in a mauve plastic cup, I walk to Charlotte's side. The machine at her side transmits a steady beat that's slightly muffled, like it's underwater. I pray with everything in me for a couple minutes, then drop a concerned kiss on my friend's head like the one I gave her mother.

I turn to the Good Doctor, who's definitely

projecting a less rumpled and more doctorly vibe today. "Call me when she wakes up. And thank you so much for staying here."

"Of course," he says, crossing his legs and picking up *The Buckneck Daily*. It's probably floundering without Tawny. I wonder if Detective Tucker stepped in and told the paper not to cover the serial killer case, since it's not a headline. Could he do that?

As if summoned by my thoughts, Detective Tucker leans into the doorway. "Mrs. Spencer?"

As I get closer, the dark circles under his bloodshot eyes become more noticeable. His camo clothing is a stark contrast with the hospital's white floors and walls. He looks like he's been camping out, and the smoky smell wafting from his hair confirms that.

"Have you been home at all?" I ask.

"Not when there's a killer like this around." He glances at his hand, as if he's itching for his Coke bottle spittoon. "Don't worry, I haven't had any chew. I keep my promises, Mrs. Spencer. That's why I'm here, matter of fact—tracked you down so I could tell you first. We've finally got a lead on this murderer. It's a link to his past. A box of letters showed up in the pit, not buried deep. I want you to read them once they're copied. I'm pretty sure they're the ramblings of a serial killer."

24

When I exit the elevator downstairs, I nearly careen headlong into someone wearing a zebra-print skirt. As my eyes travel up to her face, I recognize this particular strawberry blonde: Rosemary Hogan, the Good Doctor's daughter. The woman who once wrecked my perfectly good dress by kicking muddy water all over it.

Her wide-set eyes pin me down. "Tess Spencer."

"Rosemary."

She takes a pull on her skinny cigarette and puffs smoke to the side. "I came to see your chum, Charlotte. What in tarnations happened to her?"

I take a long look at Rosemary. She's like Marilyn Monroe with a truck and an attitude. Much as I dislike her, she should know about this killer, since she tends to draw attention.

"First of all, you need to put that cigarette out

before you set off the hospital sprinklers. Second, there's a serial killer running around Buckneck. You need to be careful."

She coughs and drops the cigarette onto a tile, grinding it out with one of her royal blue heels. "You serious?"

I pull a Kleenex from my purse and pick up the charred cigarette and ash, shoving the nasty trash at Rosemary to deal with. "I don't joke about murder. Thank the Lord Charlotte escaped. I don't know how she got away from this maniac, but she did. We don't even know what he hit her with, but he hit her *hard* to gash her head that bad."

She looks genuinely apologetic. "Look, I know I haven't been the nicest to either one of you, but Charlotte is a good woman. Laid back, free-spirited...just what Dad needs. Any way I can help? I know I'm a ways out in Point Pleasant..."

For some reason, Byron springs to mind. He talked about meeting me in town. I wonder if Rosemary could do a little undercover reconnaissance for me. Then again, if he's the killer, that's putting her right in harm's way.

"I can tell that complex brunette brain of yours is working something up," she says. "Tell me."

"I'm not sure yet. Tell you what, you give me your phone number and I'll call you if I figure out a plan."

We exchange numbers and Rosemary gives me a

parting wink. "You hurry on back to that husband of yours. I declare he must be the *yummiest* man in the entire state of West Virginia. You got yourself a keeper there, Tess."

I grit my teeth as I stalk out to the SUV, recalling all too well the time Rosemary was our waitress at the Bistro Americain. She made googly eyes at Thomas and even dropped some sultry innuendo. Thankfully, he was completely oblivious, distracted by an argument we were having.

Still, she might be able to help me gather information on Byron, since I can't really get close to him at this point. For instance, where does he live? Why does he keep showing up at the Crystal Mountain Spa? Did he share some insight about the killer with Tawny?

Something tells me Rosemary could handle this job with ease, capitalizing on her feminine charms. And if Byron tried to kill her...well, I wouldn't put it past her to run him down with her gigantic truck or shove a lit cigarette in his eye. She's got a little bit of crazy in her.

If only Charlotte would wake up, maybe she could tell us something about this killer. Did she see him? Where did he strike and how? What happened? As I wind across the mountain, I pray she'll come to soon.

I stop by the police station in town. Detective Tucker told me to pick up the copies of the letters on my way home. Nothing like sitting on my own couch, chillaxing, and reading the as-yet-unpublished memoirs of a serial killer.

I finagle my SUV into a parallel parking spot, drawing from faded Driver's Ed memories to do it properly. The phone rings as I put the SUV in park, and it's Nikki Jo. Her musical, ever-cheery voice makes it difficult to feel down.

"How was Charlotte?"

I give her a brief update, and she continues.

"Honey, I know this was a humdinger of a day for you. I've already made us some pasta salad and chicken avocado pizza. Just keeping the food light in this heat. Mira Brooke finally went down for her nap. See you soon?"

After saying goodbye, I adjust my flyaway bangs in the rear-view mirror and throw on a coat of lip gloss. About time for a haircut, I'd say. Glancing at my hands, I notice my chipped red nail polish gives the general impression of bleeding fingertips. I guess it beats that time my pale blue toenails resembled frostbite.

I meet up with the friendly cop I'd talked to at The Haven. His sunburned cheeks only highlight his ruddy complexion and I figure he's been out fishing recently.

"Mrs. S! What can I do ya for?" He leans over the counter, burly muscles pulling his sleeves taut.

"Detective Tucker said I could pick up some letters. He said someone would put them on his desk."

"Sure thing. Follow me."

I figure most visitors wouldn't get a tour of the back office at the police station, but because I'm Thomas Spencer's wife, I can get farther than most in this town. I'm struck again by the level of respect police officers have for my husband. Kind of like the respect Thomas has for Detective Tucker.

The detective's office is cramped, with no window. Something tells me he enjoys that cloistered feeling far more than I would. There's a picture of his wife on the bookshelf, and she's a total knockout. She looks very sleek and urban, compared to Detective Tucker's rugged survivalist persona.

His desk is shockingly well-organized, almost like he's OCD about things. I wouldn't have expected that, either. He's far more multi-layered than I initially assumed.

The friendly officer rummages around in the inbox and finally discovers a manila envelope. "This is it," he says, handing it to me. "You helping Detective Tucker?"

"Yes, I am."

"If it's what I think it is, you need to be careful, Mrs. S. Hey—if they catch this guy, will Thomas prosecute him? When's he getting sworn in?"

These questions just remind me how little I've been able to connect with Thomas lately. I don't even know the latest on when he's stepping into his new job.

"It'll probably be in the paper. Thanks...um..." I read his badge. "Lieutenant Wickline."

"No trouble. Just be careful and keep your nose clean." He winks.

Thomas calls as I'm pulling Nikki Jo's carefully-packed food from a Chico's bag. Mira Brooke plays with Velvet in the living room. It's a little game where the cat sneaks from behind the couch, lets Mira Brooke pet her once, then bats at her hands before zipping into hiding again. Mira Brooke gets no end of thrills from my white puffball feline.

Thomas says what I don't want to hear. "I'm going to be late again. Winding up some more cases before I leave. You can bet Royston's going to squeeze every bit of work out of me before cutting me free."

I don't want to add to Thomas' burden by giving him the rundown on my day. "When's your swearing-in, babe? We haven't even gotten to talk about it."

"Next week. I'd love for you to come and bring Mira Brooke. She won't understand what's going on, but it would mean a lot to me. That way, people can meet you both."

"Sure thing. Keep your eyes on the prize."

Mira Brooke toddles over to me, ready to eat. I

nuzzle into her cheek and savor the softness of it. Someday my girl will be a grown woman in Buckneck, just like the women this guy is stalking and killing. Morbid thought, but it gives me all the more incentive to help stop this freak while he's in our town.

Charlotte should be with her mom, not lying in a hospital bed. Or she should be here, playing with Mira Brooke and reading letters with me. The dam bursts on the tears I've held back, and Mira Brooke pats at my wet cheeks. "Maa," she croons.

I pull myself together enough to feed my baby and bathe her, but deep down I'm totally falling apart. Charlotte could have *died*. She's only forty-one.

Cute as a button in her flamingo-emblazoned onesie, Mira Brooke sits in a scholarly pose as I read *Goodnight, Moon* to her. It's one of her favorite books, even at this tender age. I tuck her into the crib, praying over her as I always do. I pray she will never in her life run into this kind of evil person and that God will hedge her with protection.

And I pray that God will hedge me as I pore over these letters, so we can put a face on the seemingly invisible Buckneck stalker.

25

It's 1:13 in the morning and Thomas still isn't home yet. But these hours have given me plenty of time to read the letters and get a feel for this killer's psyche.

He's cocky and he thinks he knows it all. He's completely inconsiderate of his child. It's not clear if the child is male or female, but he or she would've been shuttled into the foster system, apparently as a teen. There aren't many clues as to locale or time period, but I'll have Detective Tucker run down anything on that Hope's Grove Commune.

This guy has a problem with women in authority over him. He doesn't like to report to women in any way, and was probably domineered by his mother or parents early in life, given what he says about them. He runs to the woods to hunt for solace. He mentions killing a deer for venison, but there's nothing to indicate he couldn't be shooting women too. In fact, there's a gap where his child's mother goes missing and I'm betting she was one of his first victims. He broke up his family, he lost a couple jobs, and then he finally snapped.

He talks about frequenting West Virginia to hunt. He mentions land his great-grandpa owned before there was a mine on it. Maybe we can look into that lead. My dad would know—he knows every coal mine in the state, having worked the mines most of his life. But I don't know where my dad is and Junior Lilly isn't the kind who likes to be in contact with his relatives.

Even in the soft night breeze, chills run up my arms as I reread some of the letters, written in black ink on college-ruled notebook paper. The tone of the advice...that's what bothers me. It's domineering, almost brainwashing. Did the poor teen start to believe Dad was full of wisdom? Did the teen actually practice bowhunting religiously, almost *as* a religion? What if the teen found out Dad was a killer and decided to follow in his footsteps? It's Stockholm Syndrome-eerie.

That would mean our killer could be more than one killer. It could be a team.

The front door locks start moving. I know it's Thomas, but I eyeball my Glock on the coffee table, making sure it's handy.

Sure enough, my poor man walks in, obviously wiped out. His eyes are bleary and he does a double-take when he sees me on the couch with the Glock nearby.

"Was there trouble?" he asks. In the past, we've had some unhinged stalkers in our woods, so sitting up late with a gun isn't without precedent.

"Just helping Detective Tucker." I tuck my hair behind my ear, focusing again on the letters. "Hey hon, I have something I need you to look up before you leave the office: the deed for the land Dani Gibson bought."

He nods, pulling the milk out of the fridge and pouring himself a huge glass. "Any cookies?"

"None right now. But there's still a little apple crumb pie on the counter behind you."

He helps himself and plops on the couch beside me. After neatly devouring his pie and milk, he automatically starts unloading my Glock. We have other weapons upstairs and he's saying it's time for bed.

I shove the letters back into the envelope. Maybe the box they were buried in is a clue. Did the dad bury it? The child? It wasn't there when the police initially dug the area up. It must have been deposited recently...in fact, probably today. Was it early this morning, when no one was around? Or while Dani was there? Thank goodness she got out of there. But what if someone came after that? Wouldn't take long to shovel up a little dirt and cover the box.

The bigger question is why didn't they just burn the letters? Why make a lame attempt to bury them, knowing cops were monitoring the area? Nothing adds up.

Thomas notices my intense look and starts massaging my head with his long fingers. My brain goes into shutdown mode. I relish my much-needed head-rub for a few more seconds, then kiss him before we tiptoe up to the bed in silence. We've both put in more than a full day's work and it's time to sleep.

I wake up early with Mira Brooke's cries. She's not wet or hungry, so in an attempt to get her back to sleep, I let her snuggle between us. When Thomas wakes an hour later, she crawls up to hug him. But instead of lying back down easy, she crashes back, whapping her head into my eye.

"Oh!" Thomas gasps. "That must have hurt! I'm so sorry. I'll go get some ice."

From the way this aches, my eye is going to bruise big-time. This will be a hard one to explain. I picture myself attending Thomas' swearing-in, wearing my favorite mint-color dress and sporting a shiner no one believes came from my baby. Not the best first impression.

After bringing me a bag of frozen peas for my eye, Thomas kisses my forehead and Mira Brooke's tousled curls. "Love my pretty girls. I gotta hit the shower and run. You want me to fix you coffee?"

"No, I'll get my own. You go ahead and get going."

Craving a little extra sleep, I try to get Mira Brooke to calm down, but she's having none of it. She shouts "Vev" for Velvet, and the cat obediently comes upstairs to join the party on the bed. Both are so hyper I'm betting it's a full moon.

I finally give up and take the girl and the kitty downstairs for a little frolic time in the living room. After reloading the French press and putting a kettle on, I sit by the kitchen counter, munching a stale cinnamon Pop-Tart. What's the next step? I need a plan of attack.

Detective Tucker said the oldest skeleton behind the spa dated to the 1980s. I do some quick calculations and figure if he sent those letters around the time he killed his wife, and if she was the earliest victim, the child would now be in the late thirties to early forties.

First things first. I need to get a list of victims' names from Detective Tucker. Maybe the mother's last name will link to the child, if she *was* the first kill.

Second, I need to know who owned that spa land before Dani. Hopefully Thomas can find that out for me.

Third, I need to find out if that box was bought or made at some specific location. That might give us a place where the killer lived or where the child lives now.

Fourth, I need to check into Byron's history. In particular, I want to know if he was ever in foster care. That's something Rosemary can do without putting herself in harm's way. She can just walk into the computer repair shop and drop some questions, all innocent-like.

Fifth, I want to find out more about Teeny. I don't know how. I would ask Dani, but she's another one I need to check into and I can't fully trust her. Why did she move here from California? That would easily fit the profile of this murderer's child.

I try not to think of the child as "the demon seed" but the term keeps jumping to mind. Anyone with a dad like that has to be more than a little messed up.

But over all these things, I need to keep checking in on Charlotte and Miranda. I would never leave my sick friends in the lurch. And if Charlotte wakes and could give us some information, all the better.

I give Mira Brooke her favorite breakfast of Fruit Loops and bananas, since she balked the last few times I've tried to feed her oatmeal. So much for my crunchy, organic-mom dreams. They crashed to the ground pretty early in the game.

I call Detective Tucker. He must be surrounded by birds, because blue jays screech in the background. "Where are you?" I ask.

"You don't want to know. You figure out anything from those letters? I didn't have much time to mull them over, but what came through loud and clear is that he was a lazy, selfish so-and-so."

"I did and we can talk about it—how about tonight? You want to come over for coffee and dessert? The only thing I need from you is a list of names on those skeletons. I have some other details I'm working on and I'll report to you as soon as I know anything."

"Sounds like a plan. But you stay safe as you formulate these ideas. You in the little cottage behind Roger and Nikki Jo's?"

"Sure am. Could you come over around seven-ish?"

"That'll work."

I've just pulled out Mira Brooke's favorite wooden blocks and started building a teetering tower when Detective Tucker calls again—a red flag there's a bomb about to drop. And drop it does.

"Mrs. Spencer, I promised to keep you in the loop with any developments. I just caught Teeny in the woods. I haven't called Ms. Gibson yet because I don't have a handle on her relationship with him. I'm thinking if you came up here, he might talk to you before we take him in."

26

Sensing the urgency in the detective's voice, I throw on my holey, comfy jeans and a bland gray T-shirt. Grabbing the diaper bag and Mira Brooke, I head up to the big house. Sure enough, Nikki Jo has finished her workout and she's raring to babysit.

After spending a little time explaining my quickly-bruising eye, I cross-question her to make sure watching Mira Brooke won't intrude into her plans for the day.

"Goodness knows the only thing I was fixing to do today was weed the flowerbeds, and I can do that with Mira Brooke—can't I, cutey?" She tickles Mira Brooke's bare feet. "And then I'm gonna call up Andrew and see if he can make it for his brother's swearing-in. He ought to be here for that, don't you think?

A pang shoots through me. I wasn't able to say

goodbye to Andrew or Stella. I wonder how they're getting on now they're back in college, but something tells me it's another one of Andrew's ill-fated relationships. A girl who doesn't love guns in the Spencer family wouldn't be an issue, but a girl who shows disdain for those who *do* love them? Not gonna fly.

"I hope he can come," I say. Nikki Jo's dark eyes meet mine and understanding flashes between us. I didn't mention Stella and neither did she.

"We'll keep on praying he finds the right girl," she says. "Because goodness knows our Andrew always needs a girl on his arm."

I kiss Mira Brooke and rush to the SUV, spinning out a bit as I climb the steep driveway. This thing is a bear to plow in winter. Thankfully Roger is friends with just about everyone who owns a tractor in Buckneck, so there's never any question our driveway will get scraped off. It's just a question of *when*.

As I round the familiar curve topping out at the Crystal Mountain Spa, I spot Teeny on the front patio, arguing with a police officer. Good lands, that guy is going to bury himself. What was he doing out in the woods today? I assumed Dani canceled all the appointments this week. Maybe Teeny booked another secret massage.

When I pull to a stop, Detective Tucker emerges from his Hummer. He hasn't showered in a while, but apparently his camping expedition has paid off.

"Mrs. Spencer, good of you to come." He takes in my blackening eye but doesn't say one word. "You might be able to help us talk to Teeny." He glances at his officer, who's standing rigidly while Teeny shakes a fist at him. "That masseuse there is in a heap of trouble, but not the kind we'd hoped for. He's cultivated a mighty fine patch of marijuana back in the woods. He tucked it behind a thick hedge of blackberries and brambles, so I never thought to look in there."

I replay Teeny's remark when the police cars showed up at the spa. *"But this place was supposed to be safe."* Teeny had probably had run-ins with the cops before. The question is, did Dani set him up with a job here, knowing his history?

"I'll try to get him talking," I say. Detective Tucker nods, following a discreet distance behind me.

"Teeny!" I shout, waving. The officer steps aside when he notices Detective Tucker. I walk up to my co-worker with more confidence than I feel and pat his massive arm. "What's going on?"

"Tess, what are you doing here? What happened to your eye?" He doesn't give me time to answer. "Aw, shoot. The po-po thinks I'm growing pot out in the woods. Would you tell them they're wrong?"

"I don't know, Teeny. I mean, were you? What was up with those sneaky appointments at the spa? Those look suspicious, dude."

I'm lapsing into the video-game talk I use when I play Petey. But it seems to be getting through.

"Naw...oh, man, my momma is going to hit the roof."

"I'm sure she won't mind if you come clean. They'll have mercy on you if you tell the truth."

I'm not sure if that's actually the case, but his eyes soften when I mention it. Sometimes my ability to embroider the truth astonishes even me.

He leans way down and whispers in my ear. "You gotta understand, it ain't my pot. No way. But it's my momma's. I just checked in on it for her." A big tear slips down his face and he puts his arm around me. Both the officer and Detective Tucker look like they're ready to point and shoot, should the need arise. Teeny could probably crush me like a twig.

He stares at me with those deep-set, ferret-like eyes. He whispers again. "I gotta come clean. I locked you all in that sauna—it was me, Tess. I had to. I'd planned to sell some of Momma's stuff, then you and Dani came and what was I supposed to do? I had to make that sale. You don't know my momma."

Something tells me I don't want to meet her, either. I'm fairly certain Detective Tucker heard Teeny's entire whispered confession. It rots, but Teeny probably isn't our bowhunting serial killer, since he's got his hands full tending his momma's "garden."

I have one more question. "Was Dani aware of

this...sideline of yours?"

He blinks rapidly. "Nope."

"You sure about that?"

He glances at the others. "Sure am. Listen, what about Momma?"

Detective Tucker gives me a questioning glance, and I nod. I think we've reached the end of Teeny's sob story. As the detective steps forward, Teeny's arm wraps a little tighter, pressing me against his sweaty side.

"Now don't do anything stupid," I say. "This isn't the death penalty. *Unless* you do something stupid."

Teeny breaks into a full-on wail, his hands flying to his face to squish the tears away. In that moment, I race into the yard.

Both guns come out, aimed at Teeny. "Hands in the air!" the officer shouts.

Once they march him to the police car, Detective Tucker returns to my side. "I'm glad you were able to get that information from him. He'll crack under pressure and confess. The one I really need to get my hands on is his mom—the brains of this operation, I'm sure."

As the officer drives Teeny away, another question hits me. Was Byron a part of this? Maybe he was buying from Teeny and that would explain his keen interest in hanging around the spa and his personal visit to "settle the score." I mention the idea to Detective

Tucker and he says they'll ask in interrogation.

"You'd better tell Dani," I say. "Although I wonder if she didn't know about the pot. She's always been weird and kind of...over-interested in how Teeny spends his time at the spa."

"Duly noted." He gives me a weary look. "What a dead end. I'd hoped the killer would show up out there. Instead I find a pothead."

"The pot actually explains a lot about Teeny's behavior," I muse. "At least we eliminated one of my suspects."

Detective Tucker smiles, his brown-black eyes holding mine. "You have a list?"

"Just in my head, but yes."

As he looks off toward the woods, a sudden nervousness twists my stomach. We're standing here, alone. This man is armed and he knows the woods like the back of his hand. According to Nikki Jo, he's an accomplished marksman.

The picture of his lovely wife flashes to mind and I talk myself down. He's a family man. He's been camping out here, trying to catch this killer. We share the same hunger for justice. He's not a threat.

But if he were, he'd be the one threat I wouldn't see coming.

27

I confirm we're still on for dessert and coffee tonight, so I can get my hands on that list of victims' names. Then I head out to make my rounds, planning to check on Charlotte first, then Miranda.

On the way, I call Rosemary and put her on speaker phone.

"Hey, Tess. Any word on Charlotte?"

"Not yet—I'm heading over now. Listen, I thought of a little something you could do for me. You still live over toward Point Pleasant, right?"

"Have to, since I work in town. Still waitressing at the bistro."

I smile, knowing she's their star waitress. "I just need you to visit a shop—D&R Computer Tech?"

"I know that place. Right on my way. Blue awnings. What do you want me to do?"

I explain how I need her to get friendly with

Byron, then somehow find out if he's been in the foster system. Also, if she can ask if he bowhunts, that would be an added bonus.

"I know a little something about foster parents," she says. "I had the best in the world."

I've met Rosemary's foster mother, Mrs. Hogan. She's a woman with an Irish brogue and a heart of gold. "Tell your mother hello for me, and tell her I did have a baby girl, just like she guessed." I say goodbye, hanging up as I reach the hospital.

Once parked, I remember to unload the Glock and store it in the car case, so I can comply with the hospital's no-gun policy. It's almost like missing an appendage now, walking around with an empty holster. As I pass the tiered water fountain out front, I can't shake the feeling I'm being watched. Or rather, *stalked*, like an animal.

Upstairs, I peep into Charlotte's room, bracing myself to find her asleep. But the first thing I see is her bright eyes, looking my way. I give a little shout and run to her side, lightly hugging her.

"You're okay!"

She grins, her lips still cracked and pale. "You didn't think I'd be that easy to kill, did you? And what happened to you?"

My hand flies to my eye. "Must look pretty bad? Mira Brooke is what happened. Cracked her head into me...hurts like the dickens when I think about it. But enough about me. Thank the Lord you're alive, Charlotte."

"I have thanked Him, many times. But how's Mom?"

"About the same. I was going to visit her after this."

"Don't worry about it. Bartholomew will see her on rounds tonight and he'll keep me updated till I get out of here. It'll probably be in a day or two. Mercy only knows what this little hospital trip will cost me."

"Good thing you have insurance, girl." It's so wonderful to see that light in her eyes, to hear her smooth voice. "Oh! I have something to tell you about Teeny. I'm afraid he can't be your boyfriend after all."

"Shoot fire! Tell me all about it."

Half an hour passes as I fill Charlotte in on the latest in the investigation. Finally, I fall silent.

She grips my hand. "I know what you're wondering. Did I see the guy?" She sinks back into her pillow, and I fluff it behind her head, careful not to brush the wrapped wound. She focuses on the ceiling. "I don't think I did. It all happened so fast and my memories are taking their good old time coming back. But he must have snuck up behind me in The Haven parking lot. I remember this sharp pain and reaching back and feeling something sticky in my hair. Then somehow he got me into a car trunk. Maybe I passed out on the ground, I don't know."

"A trunk? Just like we practiced?"

She smiles. "Good thing we did, too. I came to and it was dark, but the car was moving and I knew I was in its trunk. I started feeling for the tail lights, but lo and behold, there was a glowing handle hanging down. It made it easy. So I waited until the car slowed, like it was reaching an intersection. I yanked that handle, the trunk popped up, and I kind of slung myself out of there, onto the pavement. He must have had the radio on because I was able to run off before he stopped."

"Did you get anything on the car? Did you ever see him?"

She shakes her head. "I wish I had, but I didn't have time to stop and read license plates, you know? It was a black car, I think, and I'd say it was a sedan because the trunk was pretty roomy. The only things I felt in the trunk were a blanket and an umbrella. I was so grateful there wasn't another body! Anyway, I staggered off and wound up in some neighborhood that looked safe. I remember beating on someone's door and that's about it."

"That's how they found you." I wince as I picture Charlotte, blood seeping from her head onto someone's front porch. "You kept it together well, girlie. Hey, did you know that even Rosemary came to visit you?"

She grins. "You don't say?"

I tell her about Rosemary's little sleuthing assignment to the computer store. "Hopefully she'll get some dirt."

"If anyone can smooth-talk a man, I'm betting it's Rosemary," Charlotte says.

The nurse comes in, ready to check vitals. She gives me a brief, dismissive nod.

"I'd better go. Oh! Did you like your flowers?"

"Yes, thanks so much. Bartholomew told me. I love the pink roses."

I laugh at her polite lie. "Not those, silly. Mine were a sore excuse for flowers and I promise I'll bring you some prettier ones from home. I meant those orange ones Axel sent. Pretty impressive, huh? Helps to have connections with the biggie florists in the area, you see."

The nurse shoots me another look. I wink at Charlotte. "Gotta go. I'll come over tomorrow, okay? And call if you need anything at all. Want me to check on your house?"

"Should be okay until I get back. Thanks, Tess. Give my love to Mira Brooke and the family. Tell Nikki Jo she can stop worrying about me...but tell her she's welcome to cook me a meal when I get home if that'll make her feel better."

"Oh, you know she'll be all over that."

Unwilling to say goodbye, I wave at her and linger in the doorway. She returns a weak wave as the nurse closes in with the blood pressure cuff.

My heart feels so much lighter, I could skip down

the halls. It seems things are coming together. Teeny has been busted. Charlotte is awake. I'm getting the list of names from Detective Tucker tonight so I can see if anything matches up with the letters.

Sunlight blinds me outside, but I savor its all-encompassing warmth. The burbling fountain and twittering birds add to my contentment. We will catch this killer soon, I just know it.

As I get closer to my SUV, something glints and catches my eye. Did someone attach something to my license? All my hopes melt into the ground as I realize what it is.

An arrow, shot directly into my license plate. If it rips through metal like that, what would it do to me?

28

I drive straight to the police station so they can get the arrow out and see if it matches the recent ones from Tawny and Melody. After taking time to fill out paperwork and answer a couple well-intended questions about my black eye, I'm finally cleared to return home.

I had hoped to stop by the grocery store for a cake mix so I could make Heath-bit chocolate cake, but there's no time. I'll have to make chocolate-chip cookies or something fast for Detective Tucker's visit. I need to let Thomas know he's coming, but I have a feeling Thomas will be working late anyway.

Nikki Jo meets me at the door, Mira Brooke on her hip. "Come right on back to the kitchen. I made us some blackberry cheesecake squares. Trying one of those Pioneer Woman recipes and law, if they aren't scrumptious! I'll send you some."

How is it that Nikki Jo always ministers to my spirit, not only with her words, but also with her food? She's like the total opposite of my own mother.

Mira Brooke leans over my way and I take her into my arms, kissing her repeatedly all over her flawless little face. I'm trying to forget the killer's blaring warning message. That arrow said *You're not safe* loud and clear.

After we eat a quick meal of spaghetti, I wash up Mira Brooke and get myself changed into nicer pants. Sure enough, Thomas is coming home late, so I'll be on my own with the detective. I'm pretty sure he's okay, but until we nail the killer, I can't trust him completely.

By the time the detective shows up around 8:30, Mira Brooke is already asleep due to her healthy dose of carbs. I'm wearing my Glock and Nikki Jo and Roger know who's visiting. As a final precaution, I've enlisted Petey as my personal spy. The curtains are pulled back on my living room window and Petey can see right into it with his high-powered binoculars. If Detective Tucker makes one false move...I shudder to think what will happen. Roger has a regular arsenal up at the big house and he's not afraid to use it.

We enjoy some blackberry cheesecake squares and

sip at our decaf coffee, reviewing Charlotte's recollections and lamenting that she didn't see the killer. When we finish, Detective Tucker pulls a list out of his Carhartt jacket and pushes it across the coffee table.

"Not much to go on, I tell you, but I've written their names, ages, and where they went missing. Also listed any remaining family members we could find. They're listed in chronological order, starting with that first death."

Reading down the list, I can't believe how many victims there were. What triggered this person? And why did they choose these unfortunate women?

Christine Colton, age 36, missing Orange Hill Road, CA, no survivors

Penny Murphy, age 18, missing Hope Lane, CA, father and a brother still alive

Julie Snyder, age 42, missing Crystal Cove, CA, no survivors

Sofia Vasquez, age 23, missing Tucson, AZ, husband alive

Kelly Sutton, age 32, missing Delta, CO, 2 daughters alive

Christy Mann, age 46, missing Marion, KS, no survivors

Anna Fontaine, age 27, missing Oak Grove, LA, parents alive

Tammy Rogers, age 34, missing Blountville, TN, husband and son alive

Melody Carroll, age 53, from Medford, OR, killed in Buckneck, WV, husband and daughter alive

Tawny Creeden, age 42, missing Buckneck, WV, husband alive

"And there were no similarities?" I ask. "Careers? The way they looked? The way they went missing?"

"Still haven't found a pattern. The only similarity is the location of those first three murders in California and we figure he probably lived there at that time. After that, who knows? He might have moved across the US and just picked off someone new everywhere he went."

"And when were these murders?"

"Spanned from the late eighties to the early 2000s—the last in that string being Tammy Rogers—then there was a break until Melody this year."

"Wonder what stopped him? Or her."

"I still don't think it's a woman letting those arrows fly," he says. "Women killing women, much less in that violent way, would be highly unusual...though not impossible."

"It's the *not impossible* that worries me, Detective. And none of these names connect with anyone in Buckneck?"

"No. None of them had a child in the foster system, so that didn't seem to link up with the letters we found. Of course, sometimes those things can be covered up."

I sigh. Why does the trail have to be so hard to follow? "Tell me more about the first victim. That has to be a clue...why he decided to kill that first time."

"Her police record is clean, and from the look of things, she wasn't married. So I don't know how that fits with any of the women mentioned in the letters."

"But there is a Julie in California. Is she the one who worked at Woolworth's—the boss he resented so much?"

"Could very well be, but it's nearly impossible to follow-up since Woolworth's closed in the nineties and they didn't keep computer records for the most part. And we couldn't find any of her survivors to ask."

"And what about the young girl...Penny Murphy? What if she was Sea from the commune? He seemed to despise her for setting him up."

"Her father confirms she'd already left home at that time, but he didn't know where she was living. She could have easily used a pseudonym at the commune, but we're having trouble locating anyone who knows about Hope's Grove."

"The biggest question is what happened to the child? Was it a boy or girl? Did they have their father's last name? Where are they now?" I pull my sweater tighter as the breeze in the window picks up.

"My question exactly. In other words, are they in

Buckneck, continuing their daddy's mission? That's what you're wondering too, isn't it?" He raises his bushy eyebrows.

I nod and offer the detective another cheesecake square. He shakes his head, glancing at his watch. "Land sakes, it's already 10:30. I need to get home for a shower." He grins.

"I hope you can sleep in your own bed tonight. Roughing it in this heat must be tough."

"The woods are never tough for me, Mrs. Spencer. And something tells me you could handle them just fine yourself." I'm impressed by his accurate insight into how I tick.

As he stands, the door opens and Thomas comes in, swinging his tie like a lasso and whistling "Livin' on a Prayer." He stops short when he sees the detective. "Oh! Detective Tucker. Didn't realize you'd be here."

Detective Tucker smiles and shakes hands. "Your wife here treated me to some mighty fine dessert and I'm much obliged for all her help on this case."

Thomas smiles wanly, not at all enthusiastic about my participation. He rallies, though. "She couldn't be working with a finer man."

Detective Tucker dons his hunting cap. "Thank you. And my congratulations to our new prosecuting attorney."

After he pulls away, I go out on the porch and make a thumbs-up toward Petey's darkened window.

I'm fairly certain he never abandoned his spy post because his light clicks on.

When I walk back in the door, Thomas blocks the way. "Tess, I think it's time you withdrew from helping Detective Tucker."

I grab his arms and shimmy into the living room, chilled from the unusually cool night air. "I'm just doing some of the brain-work, if you'd call it that. Putting things together as best I can." I try to divert his attention. "Did you know Charlotte woke up? Our hands-on trunk escape training worked! That's how she got away."

This provides ample distraction and we discuss Charlotte's adventure for a while. By the time Thomas has eaten and snuggled with me on the couch, I decide it's too late to bring up the arrow in the SUV. As Scarlett O'Hara says, "Tomorrow is another day." I'll deal with it then.

29

Thomas leaves early for work since it's his final day. The sound of *Buffy* wakes me and I groan. Dani's heard about Teeny by now and I'm guessing she's not happy. Sure enough, she starts in on a diatribe the minute I say hello.

"What is going on up there? Why didn't Detective Tucker call me in before they booked Teeny? My spa is like a hotbed of crime. It's like I'm being sabotaged!"

If not for the drastically divergent nature of the crimes, I'd wonder myself. But pot and serial killing don't seem to have much in common, at least at this juncture. Teeny seems more like a little boy who can't stand up to Mommy...but then again, maybe that personality fits our serial killer, and that's why he's preying on women. But someone shot an arrow into my car and that person was not Teeny, because he was down at the police station.

"Could we meet? I need to talk to someone," she says. "I'm over in Point Pleasant today. You ever eaten at the Bistro Americain?"

I chuckle to myself. "Sure have. Yes, we can meet up there for lunch. They make an amazing spinach ravioli."

"I only eat their vegan stuff, but I do love their portabella bacon cheeseburger. It's tempeh bacon and cashew cheese, of course."

"Of course." Mira Brooke wriggles to life beside me, rubbing her long dark eyelashes and gearing up for a cry. Thomas put her in bed next to me this morning but I didn't even notice. I think my REM sleep starts at a weird hour. "I'll meet you at one, okay?"

I call Nikki Jo, worried about asking her to watch Mira Brooke again. I don't want to impinge on her kindness, and yet she'd be babysitting if I were still working at the spa anyway. I know she cherishes every minute with her granddaughter, but what if she's tired of it? Would she even tell me?

After an enthusiastic okay from Nikki Jo, I get us ready for the day. Knowing Dani will be impeccably dressed, I try to up my game and wear something that looks a bit more put-together than normal. What this breaks down to is a khaki skirt, white polo shirt, striped tie belt which might be totally 2003, and sandals. The entire outfit shouts prep school in Connecticut to me, but it's the best I can come up with. I put on liberal concealer and foundation to try and cover my bruised eye. Finally, I pull out my leather purse designed to hold the Glock and load that baby up. I'm going nowhere without my piece.

I hate being so distracted, but I will be until they catch this killer. No one is safe. The fact that I was targeted with that arrow is disconcerting in the extreme.

As I drive across the mountain, absently noting three random shoes pitched on the side of the road, I call the Good Doctor on speaker phone. "What's the latest? Is she doing okay?"

"Sure is. They're actually letting her out today. She'll be going over to see Miranda tonight. I thought it might be too draining, but you know Charlotte. There's no stopping her when she's determined to do something."

"Oh, wonderful! I'll stop in then. I'm heading over to Point Pleasant for lunch—actually at the Bistro Americain—but tell her I'll see her at The Haven."

"And tell Rosemary hello from me. She works lunch shift."

After I pull into an open parking spot on Main Street, I get out and catch that earthy, damp smell that means rain is on the way. The swift-moving charcoal clouds confirm it.

Inside the bistro, Rosemary grabs my arm and steers me toward Dani's booth, whispering all the way. "I met up with him. Stay after your friend goes and I'll tell you about it. And what'd you do, run into a door? 'Cause I know that ever-loving husband of yours didn't pop you in the eye." She smirks and turns before I have time to shoot her a glare.

At our table, Dani looks like a million bucks, and the sight of that swanky ivory leather purse brings questions to mind about where her money is coming from. Of course she has no husband or children to spend her income on, but still...has she been skimming a little from the marijuana business?

Her usually clear blue eyes look red, and she's sniffing. Either she has a cold or she's been crying.

"Tess. What have you been doing? Detective Tucker said you were there with Teeny yesterday. Meanwhile, he hauled me in and practically ran me through interrogation. I just don't know what to think."

I focus on the flickering candle on our table, considering my answer. What have I been doing? Trying to help the women in this town stay alive— women like Dani. I'm tired of my boss' vagueness. She wants info from me? She can share some info of her own.

"Yes, I was there. And it seems to me that you might have been aware of Teeny's gig. You seemed overly concerned about his off-the-books meetings. And Teeny once told me he thought the spa was 'safe.' Now why would a grown man use that word? I think you're holding out on me."

Dani's chin tightens and her eyes sharpen. She looks less like a vegan peacenik and more like a Marine. Such a dichotomy.

"Aren't you clever? I'll lay my cards on the table. Yes, I knew about Teeny's *previous* run-ins with the law. But I was willing to give him a chance to rehabilitate because, as you know, he's the kind of masseuse who keeps the clients returning. Never too harsh or too gentle, he instinctively knows what each body needs. It's a gift, and I was trying to encourage it so he could forget his past."

She takes a tentative bite of her vegan burger, then a couple more. My spinach ravioli is way too dry but I choke down a few bites, aware of Rosemary's hawk-eyes on me.

Dani continues. "Teeny was involved in drugs for a brief time in Kansas. I see that look on your face. Yes, people do use drugs in Kansas. He dealt a few drugs, got busted, then slunk back home to mommy. But as you probably guessed, Teeny's mom is the last woman you'd want in charge of your rehab. When he applied for the job, I knew I was taking a risk."

I nod, sipping at my sweet tea. Yes, this all makes sense. It explains Dani's watchful gaze on Teeny and Teeny's disappointment when cops showed up at the spa. But I have a few more questions to ask.

"Dani, just wondering. Were you ever a foster child?"

Her beautiful face crinkles and freezes, as if she's twenty years older. "No, why?"

She's lying and I know it. "I'm just asking everyone for a project I'm working on. Was Teeny a foster child?"

"I don't know. It's entirely possible, I guess. You'd have to ask him." She eats a couple sweet potato fries, then gulps at her water. I continue with my questioning, relentless.

"And did you say you shot with bows in the Marines?"

"What does this have to do with anything? Of course you can't suspect I killed those women!"

"I didn't say that. I just asked if you shot with bows in the Marines."

"Yes, a few times. But that was so long ago and I was different then."

I lean across the table, dropping my voice. "Is your family wealthy?"

Dani glares at me. "Well, aren't we Miss Nosy-Pants today? As a matter of fact, yes. My family is wealthy and they helped me buy the spa. Are you happy now?"

"That is helpful. Thank you for being honest." Although I know that wasn't totally the case.

She stands, ice in her eyes. "I'm finished here. I wish you well with whatever you're doing, Tess. But don't you plan on having a job when I re-open.

Remember that time I said I had your back? I meant it. I don't bail on my friends, just like with Teeny. Now I'm not even sure you're my friend."

As soon as she stalks out the door, Rosemary glides over to my table, the eyes of several male customers following her. She situates herself in Dani's abandoned chair.

"Whew, she's some piece of work, isn't she? Where'd you meet that broad?" Rosemary taps her fingers on her lips, gripping an invisible cigarette. She doesn't give me time to answer. "So look here. I went to that computer shop and asked him those questions. He had a hard time staying focused...*men*, you know. Anyway. He wasn't a foster kid and he doesn't shoot bows. That's what he said."

I sigh. "But just like Dani—the woman I had lunch with—who knows if he's telling us the truth? Digging into the past is taking too much time. It seems like we need to reel this killer in fast, you know? Before there's another murder?"

Rosemary nods. Her boss calls her back to work. She smiles, which is quite disarming considering she rarely smiles at me. "Catch you around, Tess Spencer. And take care of that eye."

I walk out into the pouring rain, careening into a brick wall of a man. Axel.

30

Axel catches my arm, swinging me back under the restaurant awning. He runs a large hand through his hair, shaking some of the water out. He examines my face and frowns. "What has become of your eye?"

"It's a baby thing. You wouldn't understand."

He looks confused, then offers a hesitant smile. "Your friend liked the bouquet?"

I wish I could scold him because his orange roses showed up everyone else's flowers. Instead, I put aside my pride. "Yes. They were perfect."

"Ah, *gut*. I am going into this restaurant. You are still hungry?"

"*Nein*. I mean, no. I'm not. I just ate."

He leans against the wood door, totally blocking anyone who might want to exit. "You are checking in on your elderly friend today perhaps? Miranda Michaels?"

I didn't realize he knew her name. "Yes, I'm visiting her tonight. Her daughter Charlotte will also be there, because she's getting released from the hospital."

He gives me a look I can't describe. It's something like concern but it goes deeper. "Miranda Michaels has helped many people."

I have no sweet clue what he means, since I doubt she's helped him. Yet certainly it's true. She held me back from the brink of suicide once. But he knows nothing about that...

"*Guten Tag*," he says, swinging the door wide and charging in. I can imagine Rosemary rushing over to show him to a table. I wonder if she's his type. A hidden puddle by the sidewalk surprises me when I sploosh right into it. As I climb into the SUV, muddy water slops from my shoes onto the floor mat. Not the best day to be outside. I wonder if Detective Tucker is hunkered in a makeshift tent in the woods.

Ready to change into something dry, I head straight home. On the way, I call Thomas to remind him to check on that Crystal Mountain Spa deed before he leaves the office. Hopefully that will shed some light on who might have had access to the woods in the eighties and nineties.

Charlotte calls me as I'm rounding the final curve. "Could you come to The Haven?" Her voice is quiet and shaky. "Mom isn't doing well at all and I could really use you here."

"On my way." I pull into the closest graveled turnoff spot and reverse direction, back toward town. The water sluicing over my wipers mimics my mood. It's like I'm watching a flood approach and there's nothing I can do to hold it back.

The nurse opens the door to Miranda's suite, revealing Charlotte clinging to Bartholomew's hand on the couch. She turns her head slowly, as if a sudden twist would pain her. Her hair is still missing in a patch on the back but she looks tragically beautiful, like a Klimt painting.

I rush over to her side, hugging her. "It's going to be okay."

"She's dying, Tess."

"I know. That's why it's going to be okay. You know how much she's missed your dad. Now she will see him again...and her Savior. She's not afraid."

"I know..." Charlotte's voice fades. "But I am. I don't know how to handle any of this. I still haven't even really processed Dad's death."

The Good Doctor wraps an arm around Charlotte, somehow making the tall woman appear small. "We will do everything we can to make her comfortable. She won't be in pain. Believe me, she knows you're here, even if it doesn't seem like it."

Charlotte's lustrous eyes fill with tears. "You can go in and say goodbye, Tess."

Suddenly I'm not just the comforter, I need comfort. Remnants of our long discussions piece themselves together like a quilt in my mind. Times when Miranda encouraged me that I was special, that I had value even when no one else seemed to care who I was. Long chess games played in the dwindling summer twilight. And the laughter...oh, mercy...the laughter!

I creep in, watching this tiny woman who has been weakened, but not destroyed, by strokes and heart attacks. She never once complained about being in a wheelchair. She simply made the best of it. I truly pray I can be half the woman she is when I am her age.

Miranda takes shallow breaths, making me fearful. The nurse sitting in the corner gives me a reassuring nod. I take Miranda's hand, whispering to her. "It's me, Tess. Just wanted to..." Words don't come, but the tears do. Taking the Kleenex the nurse offers, I sit and hold my friend's cold hand, wishing I could will the strength back into her. Yet I know it's almost her time. She would tell me that herself. She'd say, "Tess Spencer, you stop that blubbering and let me go. It's time for me to get on up to Russell. He's missed his fireball wife. And law! I can't tell you how ready I am to use these legs again!"

I close my eyes and imagine Miranda young and

healthy, like she looked in pictures. Reddish-brown hair and deep blue eyes, with fair skin...like Snow White.

Finally, the nurse taps my shoulder and I glance at the clock. Time has flown. I need to give Charlotte time with her mother. I give one final squeeze and for an instant, she seems to squeeze back.

The Good Doctor has poured us both strong coffee, and I sip at it, grateful for its comforting smell and warmth. He looks closer at my bruised eye. "What happened?"

"Daughter backed into it." I don't feel like elaborating.

He nods, his battleship gray eyes swiftly returning to Charlotte. I feel a little zing as I realize he's totally smitten with my best friend. Maybe he's the only one she really needs right now, with his bedside manner and familiarity with the death process. Chances are I might make things harder by being here and crying my eyes out when she goes.

"I should probably get home," I say.

Charlotte turns to me, brimming with sadness but determined to keep her chin up. The poor girl has been through so much in this past week. "You need to go?"

"I'll stay if you want. But maybe I should go check on your house?"

She looks at me closely, seeing through my excuses yet understanding, as she always does. "Sure, if you could. I won't get back there tonight."

"You need anything at all? Clothes? Food?"

Bartholomew cuts in. "Rosemary is actually bringing us food tonight from the bistro."

I'm impressed with Rosemary's sudden interest in Charlotte's well-being. "Sounds like it's covered for now." I go over and give Charlotte a hug, wishing I could soak up some of her sorrow. "I'll be over tomorrow, bright and early."

She nods and looks out the window. Rain continues to streak the panes. Heaven is weeping for us.

In the hallway, Mr. Seger rocks on his feet, humming some disjointed tune. I walk toward the front desk, but he grabs my arm. "How is your friend? And her mother?"

I don't really think it's any of his business. "They need some privacy right now."

He nods knowingly. "Death is not the end."

Something about his cavalier attitude piques me, even if he is nuts, like the aide indicated. "Yes, but it sure feels pretty final for a while."

His eyes snap with something akin to hostility. The ever-hovering aide swoops down the hall toward us, her lanky brown hair flying. "So sorry, Mrs. Spencer. Mr. Seger needs to come play bingo with the other residents. Isn't that right, Mr. Seger?" She fingers her cross necklace.

Mr. Seger levels a completely lucid glare at the aide...or perhaps he's shooting invisible lasers at her necklace, I can't tell. "You're always right, *Peggy*." He spits out her name like it's something stuck between his teeth.

I can't deal with this weirdness. "See you later." I turn toward Peggy. "And please keep him away from Mrs. Michaels' room."

Nothing seems amiss with Charlotte's house. As I pass Thomas' office, I wish I'd picked up cupcakes to celebrate his last day there. It would be nice if they'd throw a farewell party for him, but I don't think that will be the case. Royston might have to hire two people to replace Thomas, with all the work he did. So this farewell is going to cost him.

At home, I find Nikki Jo sitting on her porch, rocking Mira Brooke. From the peach slices in her iced tea to the overflowing urns of lavender that flank her pumpkin-colored front door, I could be looking at a staged photo for *Better Homes and Gardens*.

Mira Brooke toddles to me, her curls damp with sweat. "Come on in and have you some peach tea," Nikki Jo offers. "Mira Brooke wanted to be outside but it's hotter than a pistol out here."

As we step over the threshold into air-conditioned comfort, Nikki Jo turns around and gives me a look that stops me in my tracks. I know she has some kind of bad news but I don't want to ask.

We continue into the kitchen, where she methodically takes out a glass, puts three cubes of star-shaped ice into it, then pours it full of sweet tea. She passes it to me.

"Charlotte called just before you got here." Her eyes fill and tears start to smear her eyeliner. "Miranda..."

I hear what she's saying but only one thing registers—Miranda Michaels is dead. All my Scotch-Irish emotional restraint flies out the window. I bury my face in Mira Brooke's curls and weep.

31

The weekend hurtles along like a loaded coal train with no brakes. After Charlotte and I wrap up funeral arrangements, she extracts a promise that I'll stay with her for the entire wake, funeral, burial, and follow-up fried chicken meal at Nikki Jo's. Some of Miranda's distant relatives flew in to stay with Charlotte, so at least she has that distraction.

Never does the community of Buckneck band together like when it loses one of its own. Just about every woman in town sends food for Charlotte, from loaves of fresh-baked bread to huge casseroles designed to feed the entire family. I wind up transporting several things back to Nikki Jo's chest freezer to save for later. Each kind face brings fresh tears to my eyes as I realize how many lives Miranda touched, just like Axel said.

Thomas shoos me off every time I try to take over

baby duty. "You be there for your friend. She needs you. Mira Brooke and I are having daddy-daughter bonding time."

The funeral itself is a posh affair, as befits a Grande Dame like Miranda. I'm pleased that many caregivers from The Haven show up, but I'm not thrilled that Mr. Seger tagged along. As he gives Charlotte's hand an exaggerated shake and loudly whispers, "My deepest condolences, mademoiselle," I kind of want to slap him. He never even met Miranda. Plus, I don't like the way he's acting so familiar with Charlotte. I wish Thomas were around to give him a manly "back-off" glare, but he took Mira Brooke and left early to set up chairs and tables at Nikki Jo's. The Good Doctor has been sidelined by a hypochondriac patient, so it falls on me to shuttle Mr. Seger back to an aide. We finally run into Peggy, who timidly emerges from the bathroom like she's been hiding.

"Mr. Seger paid his respects." Like most Southern women, I possess the natural ability to wrap my irritation in words that don't offend, but unmistakably get the point across. "He might be getting tired."

She nods and firmly takes his arm.

"*Au revoir*, Mrs. Spencer." He gives me a little salute.

I didn't realize he knew my name, but it doesn't matter. Hopefully I'll never step foot in The Haven again. It's nothing but a storehouse of memories now.

Finally, we sing the last hymn—"When We All Get to Heaven." Charlotte and I take one final look at Miranda, looking snazzy as ever in a navy suit that would have brought out the blue in her eyes. Her hands rest on her Bible, which brings a fresh influx of tears to my eyes. That woman read and lived the Bible every day I knew her.

Companionable silence hushes the opulent interior of the Good Doctor's Lexus on our way to the cemetery. The day seems to reflect Miranda's life— brilliantly clear, with nary a cloud in the sky. The dry ground has absorbed the recent rains, so our heels don't get stuck in the grass.

As the pastor pays tribute to Miranda, I find myself hoping again that I will age like she did—not just maintaining her classy beauty to the end, but her sense of humor and her deep concern for others, as well. I raise my eyes to the sky and thank the Lord for our Miranda Brooke, a constant reminder of one of the closest friends God ever blessed me with.

Back at home, the gladiolas, roses, and lilies from church have been artistically arranged on Nikki Jo's wraparound porch, nearly choking me with their fragrance. Inside, the church women have filled the tables with mashed potatoes, rolls, green beans, fried chicken, and homemade lemonade. Charlotte and the Good Doctor begin to greet guests. I search for Thomas and Mira Brooke.

The kitchen swarms with women. Nikki Jo is at the helm, giving orders like a head chef. Balancing a cheesecake in one French-manicured hand, she guesses who I'm looking for. "They're out back!"

On the patio, I scan the growing, milling crowd for my husband, feeling on the verge of collapse. I'm sure Charlotte feels this way and worse. All I want is to get a few plates of food and go back to the cottage, kick off these heels, and decompress.

I'm about to tell an unsupervised little girl to stop chewing on Nikki Jo's lavender hosta flowers when a large hand slides around my waist. Thomas gazes down at me with Mira Brooke perched on his arm. She looks like a fairy in her violet dress.

"Are you a parking ticket? 'Cause you've got *fine* written all over you," he whispers.

I grin. "Corny, but I'll take the compliment."

"How are you holding up?" Mira Brooke kicks at his leg with her patent-leather shoe, but he doesn't flinch. My man is tough.

"Tired. How are you?"

"Hungry. How about this...you head back to the house with Mira Brooke. I'll snag some food from Mom and we can chill. This meal is mostly for the family anyway. I know you're like family to Charlotte...but Doc Cole seems attached to her these days. Are those two *together* together?"

I nod. Mira Brooke launches into my arms,

twisting my dress to one side.

"Andrew will be disappointed." Thomas grins. "Passed over for an older man."

I smile. Not only does Thomas know how to cheer me up, he also senses when I'm completely worn out. This small gesture—picking up food for us and hanging out at the house with me—touches me more than anything else could at this juncture.

"See you at home." Mira Brooke and I crunch the gravel back to the house. I'm thankful to get beyond the shrubbery that separates our yards and hides us from sight. Someone else will have to corral that wild flower-munching child. I'm going to end this day on a happy note and spend time with my family, which is just what Miranda would want.

32

After our bellies are pleasantly full of Southern comfort food, Thomas and I settle in on the porch swing. I squeeze up bites of a popsicle for Mira Brooke, whose lips are now watermelon pink.

Thomas stretches his legs, which seem twice the length of mine. "I forgot to tell you. Dani bought that spa property from a shareholder in a defunct coal company. He'd been paying taxes on the land for years. Apparently there used to be a coal mine up in those woods, but after a tragic accident, people wanted to forget about the whole business. The mine closed down back in the seventies."

As a bit of ice slips to the ground and melts into a pink puddle, I think of that twined log cross in the woods. Maybe it marked the mine? Surely some family member would want to remember where the tragedy occurred.

"Thanks, Thomas." I give him an energetic, lingering kiss.

"Woah, that's deluxe," he says. "By the way, my swearing-in is Thursday afternoon at two at the courthouse. Andrew may even come in for the occasion. We're hoping it's too last-minute for him to bring a girlfriend as his carry-on."

"I wouldn't miss it for the world."

At midnight, I pad down to the kitchen to prowl for snacks and turn up nothing but stale nacho chips and expired yogurts. Disturbing images play on a reel in my mind. The cross in the woods. The arrow in my SUV. Bones behind the spa. Death is everywhere, striking anyone from a local news reporter to my friend of many years, even though they're not connected in the least.

After finally deciding on a piece of toast with Nutella, I sit on the couch and rifle through the letters. It feels like a dead end. The police have probably checked into any clues, like the fact the letter-writer was a professor who got sacked. The early murders happened before the days of the internet and it's probably too time-consuming to hunt down a mysterious commune or to find a Woolworth's employee who went missing.

A loud clomp outside the window just about makes me jump from my skin. I run upstairs to wake Thomas, positive it wasn't an ordinary bump in the night. Skunks are out this time of year, but there's no reason they'd be up on the porch messing with our house.

I tiptoe downstairs behind Thomas, who totes his .45. I'm quietly pleased with the strength his torso conveys even in the shadowy light hitting the stairs. I don't know how he does it, but the man is nothing but lean muscle.

After flipping the porch light on, he throws the front door open. I stay inside as he uses his flashlight to check around the house. When he finally returns, confident there's no one nearby, he motions me onto the porch.

He flexes his jaw, pointing to the wall. "There's your thumping sound."

I turn slowly, realizing what it is before I see it. An arrow has torn into our wood siding, splintering a section of it like a tiny battering ram. But that isn't all. It has pinned a note to the white paint that says *You're next* in glued-on magazine letters.

Thomas' eyes reflect enough of the porch light that they might as well be on fire. I've never seen him so angry.

"I swear if Detective Tucker doesn't catch this

monster, I will, Tess. I mean I will hunt that sucker down and take his life, do you understand? No one is getting this close to my wife and child. Now get back in the house." He points the gun at the woods for good measure.

He never bosses me around like this. I feel like a fool for getting involved in this case. I should have left the spa that first day. I should have stopped poking around. Why did I think an expert stalker like this wouldn't find out where I lived?

After Thomas simmers down, he throws down a protective decree. "I want Bobby or somebody positioned at our house. Bobby Wickline—police friend of mine. And I want you sticking around, no running about or following up on anything. Nothing to do with this murderer, okay? I'll call Detective Tucker in the morning. And once I pack up the office I'll stay close to home. No one will touch you or Mira Brooke. Maybe I'll move you up to the big house with Dad and Petey. With Mom, for that matter. She could probably snipe any idiot lurking around in the woods with Dad's Socom semi-automatic."

I nod numbly. I picture myself straddling cracking ice on a sub-zero river, praying I won't plunge to my death. Move Mira Brooke up with Nikki Jo and Roger? Sure. Stay home indefinitely? No problem. I'm not risking anything. Just check my life at the door.

Reading my spooked look, Thomas pulls me into

his chest. His loud heartbeat steadies my own. He strokes my hair and prays aloud for our safety.

Hours later, curled next to Thomas' side, with our multiple front door locks secure, I give up on sleep. I slip into the bathroom and lock the door.

My past awakens, pushing one idea forward like a counterfeit savior. Pills will make this go away, a voice says. A pill will help you sleep, will make tomorrow easier. It always made Mom calmer in the midst of the hurricane that was my childhood. Come to think of it, there are a few pills left over from Thomas' tooth surgery in the medicine cabinet...

"Never." I say it aloud to the bathroom walls. I'd rather be taken out with an arrow than put my daughter through that.

33

~*~

When I wake around ten, Thomas is gone and so is Mira Brooke, but there's a note on my pillow.

Took Mira Brooke up to Mom's. You needed sleep. When you're ready, go on up for some quiche. And take your things because you're staying there for a while. Bobby is outside our front door and he'll follow you up to the big house. Love you honey and please don't be driving anywhere.

And so it begins. I'm housebound just as surely as if I were on bed-rest. I feel trapped, like an animal in the woods, which is precisely how a deranged bowhunter would want me to feel.

I call Detective Tucker as I pack to tell him about the arrow and note. He already knows, since Thomas called him around 5 a.m. to tell him he wanted somebody posted here and that he wanted me off the case.

"I understood his concern and I agreed with him. Obviously you're the next target, Mrs. Spencer, and we aren't taking any chances."

"Well...will you tell me when anything turns up?"

"Nope."

"Couldn't you tell me if there are any more murders?"

"Nope. I'm not breaking my promise to your husband. I want to have a good working relationship with the new prosecuting attorney. You sit tight and go to Mr. Spencer's swearing-in on Thursday. I've called in a few reinforcements from neighboring counties and an FBI investigator is flying in tomorrow. One way or another, we're going to bag this killer."

"Detective Tucker...let's just say this murderer did somehow get to me. You're a hunter. How do you avoid getting hit with an arrow? I mean, is he shooting these women at close range? Hunting them from the trees?"

"From what we can tell, it's usually from around ten to twenty yards, which is the average range for a deer hunter. The first two victims had angled arrow entries, so we figure he shot them from a tree or platform. But the rest are straight shots, so he's been near ground level with the later victims—maybe in a blind of some kind."

"And there's nothing you've turned up in the woods? Did you check the area with the homemade wood cross?"

"I did and I found nothing out of the ordinary, but I'll check that area again. You need to stop pondering these things. I want you to stay alive, Mrs. Spencer. For your husband's sake and your child's—and for Nikki Jo and the family."

After hanging up, I shove the envelope of letters into my tote, thinking of the sickness filling the pages. One phrase that springs to mind is: *"We will truly make an unstoppable team."* Did this strange father and his child eventually become a team? That could explain the frequency of the attacks in this area.

Nikki Jo texts me, pulling me from my bleak thoughts.

Hey honey were eating quicksand for brunch and you are welcome to join us. Charlotte is coming over around noon to chalk. There is a cot outside your door.

I call her back to let her know I'll be up, hoping my grin isn't detectable on the phone. It cracks me up that she doesn't check these messages before sending, but deciphering her unintentional blunders has brightened my darker days.

As I walk out, Lieutenant Wickline offers to help me with my bag. Immediately all the crime dramas I've ever seen fly through my head. If anyone is the serial killer, it must be him. He's insinuated himself into my life so he can get close enough to kill...

But of course he's holding no bow or arrows and I'm being ridiculous. Still, I decline and haul my own stuffed bag up to the big house. Thor throttles down the path to greet me, and for once I'm glad for the exasperating critter's company. I'd bring Velvet up but Roger is allergic to her. Thomas will look in on her while I'm holed up with the Spencers.

Mira Brooke speed-toddles my way when I get in the door. Nikki Jo is close on her heels. "Lawsie, but this gal has ants in her pants today! I figure she'll be plum wore-out by the time Charlotte gets here." Her voice takes on a subdued tone. "She's having a hard time getting rid of those do-less relatives of hers. They won't lift a finger to wash a dish. I told her to stop cooking for them and we'll see how long they stick around."

"Good advice." I pick up Mira Brooke and swing her around.

"Roger went golfing...of course it's right when I need him to dig up a hole for my new orange rhododendron. You ever seen one of those? It just beats all." Suddenly she lays a hand on my arm, as if to steady me. "I guess you heard there's another woman missing?"

I pull Mira Brooke close to my chest, like I need to

protect her from what Nikki Jo's saying even though she can't understand it.

"No. Who was it?" I was supposed to be next. Maybe the killer gave up on targeting me...or maybe the poor woman was snatched before the killer shot that warning note into my house.

"Don't know. Far as we know it's no one from church. Goldie put it on the prayer chain soon as she heard it on the scanner. They haven't released names yet."

Quite a few people have police scanners in these parts, to keep up with the local news. It's a lot faster than the newspaper, but maybe not quite as lickety-split as the prayer chain.

We lay out dishes and coffee cups for brunch. Petey bops into the kitchen, swiping a leftover blueberry muffin before his friends pick him up for bowling. His cavalier attitude makes it apparent that Nikki Jo hasn't divulged the real reason why I'm staying at their house.

"Glad you're hanging out up here, Tess. When I get back let's play a few matches. Although I'll warn you, I've leveled up about twenty times."

"You'll make me look like a newbie."

"It's *newb*," he corrects.

"Whatever—the point is, I am one now, compared to you."

He smiles broadly. "We'll still have fun. I'll cover

you."

As he canters into the dining room, those last words remind me of Dani. She said she'd have my back and she seemed to mean it...at least until I insulted her with my probing questions. Now I have no job to return to, once this confinement is over.

I meet Charlotte on the porch. She looks more tired now than she did in the hospital. Taking Mira Brooke into her arms, she nuzzles into my girl's curls and whispers "sweet Miranda Brooke" over and over. Mira Brooke's shining eyes take on a sober look, almost as if she understands Charlotte's grief.

Nikki Jo serves up the sausage and red pepper quiche, apologizing that the top got too brown, but we all know it'll taste like something you'd pay big bucks for in a restaurant. As Nikki Jo brews a second pot of coffee, Charlotte sighs. "Maybe I should move in here too. I have so much to do and these house guests aren't helping."

"What do you have to do? Tess and I might could help," Nikki Jo says.

"Mostly, I have to go through Mom's things over at The Haven. They have a fast turnaround there and they've already booked the suite for an incoming resident. Bartholomew and his friends loaded up the furniture and hauled it to my shed, but now I need to go through clothes and books and...everything else."

The most emotionally grueling things, no doubt. Just the sight of Miranda's favorite sweater might send me over the edge. But there's no way I can leave my friend to do this alone.

"If Mom will watch Mira Brooke, I'll help you out," I say. Nikki Jo and Charlotte both give me that *oh-no-you-didn't* look.

"You know Thomas doesn't want you stepping foot outside our house," Nikki Jo says.

"I know. But it's just The Haven. I'll ride with Charlotte, we'll get the job done, and come straight back here. Shoot, I'll even take Bobby the police officer along if it makes everyone feel better. But I am *not* leaving Charlotte in the lurch on this."

"You sure you don't mind going back?" Charlotte toys with her quiche crust, politely avoiding my eyes.

"I didn't plan on it, but this is the last thing you need to tackle by yourself right now. It'll give us both closure, you know?"

She nods, a tear escaping her long lashes and splashing to her plate. "Thank you," she whispers.

Fresh determination fills me. "I'll call Thomas when I'm coming home, Mom." I know Nikki Jo is conflicted about letting me go, but her desire to do right by Miranda's girl wins out.

"You do that, honey. And you'd better tell that police officer what you're up to."

From the catch in her voice, I can tell Nikki Jo is worried the stalker will return, and no wonder.

"I'll tell him, but I want him to stay here with you." My mother-in-law and baby girl will stay safe at all costs.

34

~*~

We pick up boxes and packing tape from Charlotte's house, where her relatives are munching on donuts someone must have dropped off. Maybe I should tell Nikki Jo to put the word on the Buckneck streets that no more provisions are to be delivered to Charlotte's house. I'm pretty sure her moochers will high-tail it out of here when the mouth-watering meals stop. The kitchen looks like a dive, but everyone seems content to eat in the midst of the disarray.

I'm about to make a snarky remark in the effort of shooing them off faster, but something restrains me. They came to honor Miranda, and I appreciate that. Then again, I don't remember any of them visiting Miranda when she was alive...but I'll bite my tongue. Being the longsuffering type, Charlotte probably won't say anything to them directly, unless they stay into August. I, on the other hand, am happy to broach the subject of their immediate evacuation, however impolite it might be. It actually seems pretty impolite on their part to move in with a grieving daughter.

Charlotte reads my ominous look and scoots us out to the car quickly. "It's okay. I got this."

"You do? Because it looks like they've more than made themselves at home in there. Do they have jobs?"

"They do...and so do I, remember? I have to head back to WVU in August."

"You're going back? But...you just got out of the hospital. Your mother just died. You need time."

"I need no such thing. The best thing for me is to throw myself into teaching. I love the feel of wet clay in my hands. I love watching students' excitement as they realize they can make something elegant out of a cold gray lump. I have to go back, Tess."

I want to shout, "And leave me?" but I don't. "Who will take care of your mom's house? Will you come back in summer?"

She smiles. "All these questions. For now, let's focus on the task at hand."

We ride the rest of the way in silence. As we awkwardly haul the flattened boxes through the hallway of The Haven, I feel an urge to run right out the front door. I don't want to see Miranda's suite again.

Charlotte unlocks the door and swings it open. There's not a stick of furniture left. The room should seem cold in its starkness, but there is enough of

Miranda left to alleviate that effect. Her furs and sparkly dresses hang in the closet...her glasses sit on the pile of books in the living room. She doesn't need those glasses anymore. I swipe at my fast-forming tears.

As I start arranging books in a large box, Charlotte shakes her head. "That'll be too heavy. Books go in smaller boxes."

"Sorry. It's been years since I've packed. I've forgotten all the logistics." I take the books out, determined to be a help to my friend.

Hours pass in relative silence, both of us swirled up in memories of Miranda Michaels. Her numerous biblical commentaries and Bible notebooks remind me of how close she walked with God. I feel so inadequate in the face of her faith, but I know she'd tell me we each grow at our own speed and the point is to be *growing*.

Bartholomew drops off food from Wendy's when he comes to round at The Haven. As Charlotte leans into the Good Doctor's shoulder, I'm surprised again that this relationship works. The twenty-plus years between them doesn't seem to make one whit of difference. I turn back to my packing but a sudden pang of longing for Thomas waylays me. I'll call him before I leave so he won't worry.

As we sit on the floor and eat, Detective Tucker calls, which can't be good. Maybe they found the missing woman.

"Mrs. Spencer, I have to share two things I felt you needed to be aware of for your own safety. First of all, Dani Gibson was adopted. I found that out by tracking down her sister in Oregon—adopted sister, I should say. I'm checking into the ins and outs of it, but in the meantime, I don't want you having any contact with her, even on the phone. Second, Byron Woods was indeed in the foster system, but not in West Virginia. In Canada."

He doesn't mention the missing woman. I know he's keeping his word to Thomas to keep me out of the action. When I hang up, Charlotte and I discuss this rapid turn of events. This could mean that Dani or Byron could be the child of the serial killer.

I consider Dani first. She could have taken up her dad's stalking, bought the land in West Virginia, and continued the warped family tradition. Those brainwashing letters would infiltrate her psyche. And the casual way she slipped her arm around my neck seemed second nature to her. I shiver, picturing Dani ruthlessly coshing Charlotte's head with a brick, or hiding behind a camouflage deer blind and shooting Melody and Tawny. Her love of all things New Age does match up with the Buddhist references in the letters.

Byron's mysterious life in Canada will be tricky to check into. I wonder if they had Woolworth's and communes up there in the eighties. Byron's dad could have been a Canadian professor who traveled periodically to West Virginia. It was easier then—you didn't need a passport to cross the border. I'm almost sure it was Byron's white van flashing through the woods. He could have easily dropped the bodies off at the spa since he was often on the scene. And a male serial killer is more likely. He might have adopted his dad's derogatory attitude toward women, which shone through in the letters.

Charlotte pats my hand. "Don't stress. Everyone is looking out for you. Besides, I think you're tougher than either one of them."

By the time we've packed everything, it's dark out. We certainly aren't the fastest movers, but that wasn't really the point. The point was going through Miranda's things and saying goodbye.

Charlotte stretches, like a lean jungle cat. "We'll leave the boxes here and Bartholomew and his friends will pick them up tomorrow. I'll need to close things out with accounting and let them know they can clean now. Would you mind going over the floors with a broom real quick? They have a big one down at the end of the hall in the janitor's closet."

"No problem. Then I'll help you carry those boxes of Miranda's personal things out to the car."

The hallway lights have been dimmed, so as not to keep the residents awake. It seems surreal that this is probably the last time I'll be in this building. I remember the first time I met Charlotte, in the dining room here. I was so sure I'd hate the city girl who had been overseas when her mother needed her. Instead, she quickly won me over, as she does everyone.

I open the door and feel for a light switch. Flipping it on, I scan the organized space for the broom and finally locate it behind a Lysol-laden metal shelf. When I grab it, something catches my eye. A shoe. I look closer. The shoe is attached to a body—a woman's body with an arrow through her chest and a dirty mop bucket casually covering her head.

Taking the broom handle, I hesitantly poke at the yellow bucket. It dislodges easily, revealing a terror-stricken face I won't soon forget. Peggy. The aide who was constantly shepherding Mr. Seger.

I turn to run to the front desk, but only make it one step before my world goes black.

35

When I come to, I recognize the wet, cool rock smell around me. My childhood comes back in a flash—the smell on daddy's boots, infused in his beard. The black smell of coal.

My hands are duct-taped in front of me, but that was a big mistake on my kidnapper's part. I just watched a video about how to get out of duct tape when my hands aren't behind my back. Lifting my hands over my head, I thrust them down toward my legs, each hand pushing toward its respective side. Sure enough, the tape rips and I'm free. I don't waste time reveling that the move worked. I need to get out of here.

Scrabbling around the dirt floor, I hit on the metal tracks made for minecarts. I can probably get out if I follow them the right way...whichever way that is. Hesitantly, I touch the nape of my neck, which is pounding. There's a huge goose egg there, but no bleeding. Still, it can't be good that I was out for so long. This mine is probably deep in the underbelly of the woods behind the spa. How the killer moved me here, I can't imagine.

Is Detective Tucker camped in this very woods, listening for things? Or is this mine in an entirely different location?

I crawl to the left, following the tracks. There's no light coming from either direction. It's dark as one of those cave tours where they cut the lights out, as if it's something entertaining. There's nothing fun about standing on a narrow wet rock ledge with nothing to hold onto, wondering if you'll slip off the side into the endless chasm below. I don't like cave tours.

Thomas said there had been a horrible accident in this mine. I picture buckled walls and I'm glad I can't see. What if I'm in a tiny space, only big enough for a minecart? I push down the claustrophobic feelings slithering up my chest. I *will* get out of here alive.

After creep-crawling for what seems like a couple of hours, I have no clue if I've edged closer to the entrance or away from it. The dark is like a blanket, I tell myself. Just a cloak to protect me from the killer. I will not panic.

Suddenly, a voice cuts into the darkness. A man's voice.

"There you are, Mrs. Spencer. I knew you were tenacious, but my, my. You've exceeded my expectations."

Is it Byron? Teeny? Neither seems to fit the melodramatic tenor voice. I don't know who this person is, or where he is for that matter.

"That trick with the duct tape was memorable. I enjoyed watching that."

Watching that? He can see me, then. And he's observing me like I'm on some sick reality show.

My hand slides to my Glock, and I'm shocked to find it's still there. He was a fool to leave it on me.

"So you realize I've left you the gun. It only makes the game more interesting, you know. Tell me, have you ever read *The Most Dangerous Game*? It's a story in which a consummate hunter grows bored with stalking large game. Game can't reason, you see. Animals rely solely on instinct and reason trumps instinct. This hunter turns his sights to more intelligent prey...namely, human beings." His dry laugh cracks into the dark like a shot. "I took up this challenge years ago and have found it never fails to disappoint. Women are the most adaptable, resourceful prey, I've found. Especially determined women like you. I saved you for last, Mrs. Spencer."

I clear my throat, hoping to get him talking so I can get a fix on where he is. His voice seems close but I think the echoing walls are producing that effect. "So I'm your last kill? I'd say you've killed enough women already."

"I planned to stop at eight, in honor of the Noble Eight-fold path of Buddhism. But I couldn't resist one last jaunt to West Virginia. I felt a need to sample its wares. Oh, I was clever going about it, I assure you. Even you fell for my ruse."

"How do I know you?" I slide the Glock noiselessly from its holster, aiming in the direction of his voice.

"Ah, but Madam Spencer, did you not sense I was not mad, as you had assumed? I have a certain dramatic flair that allows me to—"

I pray and pull the trigger, smooth as butter. Right after the blast, I hear another sound—the sound of a bullet hitting metal.

His laughter rips into the silence. "You didn't really think I'd leave myself exposed, did you? Every hunter needs to be invisible to his prey."

Once again, this maniac leaves me with no moves. I'm trapped in a lightless coal mine, unsure which direction is out. He can see me and I can't see him. I also can't risk taking another shot that might ricochet into me. Seems like my only option is to run like the wind the opposite direction of his voice, but I have no doubt he'll sink an arrow in my back if I do that. Maybe if I can keep him talking...

"So those other women...you shot them straight-on. Did they have a chance to get away?"

"Of course they did—but not really. You see, I

didn't give them quite the sporting chance I've given you. I watched their pride, their haughtiness, slip away. I saw women who had bossed me around shift into the groveling, insipid souls they really were. It is actually a refining process, come to think of it. I put them through the crucible and they melted like cheap metal."

Anger rises to the surface but I try not to let it seep into my voice. "I thought Buddhism demanded no violence."

"This was simply a higher calling. I was teaching these women they could not control people and shouldn't strive to do so. I was ending their ignorance in this life, and enlightening them for the next. They needed to understand *death is not the end*."

I stand in stunned silence. Mr. Seger. He has been giving me clues—calling me *Madam*, hinting at his dramatic ruse. The ruse was integrating himself into an assisted living home, pretending to be loony. I think of poor Peggy, so determined to keep a watchful eye on him. And yet during his "escapes" he probably killed Melody and Tawny...and finally, Peggy herself.

"Where's Peggy?" I ask, hoping to taunt him into revealing himself.

His lowered voice seems to inch closer, tickling my ear. "Peggy didn't know how to leave well enough alone. She meant well, I know. Just a miserable drone doing her job. But she got a bit too nosy. Just like you, Mrs. Spencer."

A pebble clatters to the ground behind me. It's probably a regular thing in these mines...or is it? I have to keep him talking. He fancies himself a teacher, so I'll be a student.

"The first was your wife?"

"Yes. The world needed to be purged of her ignorance, her determination to believe that God would make everything work out for our family. I *was her god* in the end, Mrs. Spencer." He pauses, adopting an uncomfortably familiar tone. "Or should I call you Tess? I have wondered how that name would sound on my lips. Your lips, by the way, remind me of a girl I once kissed. She seemed so young and naïve, so willing to learn. But she turned on me and spread lies."

"You mean Sea."

"How did you know about her? How dare you speak her name?" His voice trails off, like he's talking to himself. "The most delectable hair and baby-soft skin. She couldn't spare me one kiss..."

I want to use the moment to run, but what if I run into a wall? A drop-off? No matter what, he'll be able to shoot me easily. I'm a sitting duck. A fish in a barrel.

His voice turns gruff. "We won't tell anyone if I steal a kiss from you when you die, will we? You see, I chose you as my last kill mostly because of your husband. I understand he will be the prosecuting attorney soon and I overheard Lieutenant Wickline saying what an upright man he is. Law-abiding." He laughs.

"Yes, he is. What is that to you?"

"I have found that humans have such gaping weak spots, you see. And I love to see them squirm. I thought it would add a new dimension to my game if your husband had to prosecute the one who killed his wife."

I don't point out that Thomas would withdraw from trying that case. Or would he? I replay Thomas' words that night the arrow pinned the note to our house: "*I swear if Detective Tucker doesn't catch this monster, I will, Tess. I mean I will hunt that sucker down and take his life, do you understand? No one is getting this close to my wife and child.*"

This man wants to destroy not only me, but also my husband. And yet if I'm his last kill, my daughter and the other women of Buckneck will be safe from this cretin. But what if he changes his mind, as he did after that eighth kill?

"Women in particular are so weak," he continues. "Every one of them calling out for someone as they die. For God, for their child, for their parents...always someone. Who will you call out for, Tess?"

I cringe, unwilling to focus on dying, which is probably what he wants me to do. Contemplate my end, give up hope, and all that rot.

Yet I know in my heart what the last word on my lips will be. It will be *Thomas*.

36

~*~

I determine to play my last card to shield myself and Thomas from this man's wickedness. I pull my gun again and shoot in his general direction. Turning, I run at top speed the other way. I crash right into someone.

Someone who has been standing behind me all this time.

There are two of them.

A familiar voice slices into the darkness, breaking down any vestige of hope I was clinging to. "Daddy. I'm here."

Quiet prevails, and for one blessed moment I think I've hit him. But he croaks a reply.

"Danielle? My little girl? Is that you?" He's obviously crying.

"Yes. I have waited for this day for so long. I've finally found you."

Mr. Seger sniffs a little before launching into an

explanation. "My Danielle was named after me: Daniel Seger. I doubt she still has my last name, though. Many years ago, I had to leave her with foster parents, hoping she'd understand."

"Of course I understood. They were good to me. I was pretty ripped up that you didn't come to pick me up when I turned sixteen, but I channeled that energy and eventually joined the Marines. I honed the skills you told me I had."

I stand stock-still, hopelessly trapped between the two bowhunting killers. How can Dani—peace-loving, tree-hugging, incense-burning Dani—be part of this insanity? She told me she wanted to forget her time in the Marines. I guess she's a good actor, like her dear ol' dad.

She shifts around, taking a few steps back. I can't see what she's doing but Mr. Seger can.

"Ah! It does my heart good to see you with that crossbow, my dearest. You handle it so well. Let's get this kill over with so we can visit, what do you say? I know you don't have night-vision so I should probably take this shot. Just step back to the left, behind that wood post."

Scuffling ensues. A blinding flashlight clicks on behind me. Dani shouts, "Get down, Tess!"

I drop like a ton of bricks, not caring if I hurt myself in the process. I roll quickly to the side. A whip-thwack sounds above my head, followed quickly by a feral scream of pain.

"How do you like me now, *Daddy?*" Dani grabs my hand, pulling me up. "Come on. We can get out this way."

I'm still dazed that Dani shot her father, but I follow her flashlight beam through the tunnels. She begins to explain.

"When you finally told me those women were killed with arrows, I realized Dad had returned to Buckneck, just as I'd hoped. I had situated the spa here because it had been his special hunting spot. I wanted to set my own trap for him."

Her voice thickens with emotion. "See, I always had this suspicion he'd killed Mom. But when I told the police, they barely checked into it. They just decided she ran off. It crushed me. I was a teen, and there was nothing I could do to prove my dad was a killer. He sent me all those letters, but they never directly stated he'd killed any women. I joined the Marines to get as far away from him and my memories of Mom as I could."

She sighs. "I would have told Detective Tucker, but I didn't want to be mocked again for throwing out crazy accusations. So I hid that box of letters, hoping someone would put the pieces together. In the meantime, I didn't know where Dad was. So I started following you."

Not really comforting, but it explains why I felt

someone was watching me all the time.

"I shot that arrow into your license at the hospital, by the way. I wanted to warn you to back off, because I figured you were just the type my dad...hunted."

"And the arrow in my house? With the note?"

"Not me."

So Mr. Seger *had* been in our woods, stalking me. I shudder. "Should we go back and make sure he's dead? What if you missed?"

Dani laughs. "I didn't miss. I've trained with that crossbow for years, hoping for the day I could plant an arrow in his thick skull. You heard what he said. He admitted to killing my mom and those other women. You understand? He took my *mom* from me—the only one who loved me. He cared for no one but himself."

"But won't you be tried for murder?"

"Let me tell you something. 'It's better to be tried by twelve than carried out by six.' Have you ever heard that quote? It means it's better to shoot in self-defense and ask questions later than to have pallbearers haul your coffin out. I saw my chance and I took it."

She stops short at a wooden door. "This is it. It's another entrance I found after trailing Dad into the woods. I had time to check out the mine and hide before he dragged you down here. Even though he surprised me by returning so early, I was able to hide until I could get a clear shot."

Leaves rustle as someone runs toward us. Dani

steps out, releasing my hand. I hunker back into the mine, not prepared to meet another challenge.

Detective Tucker stretches a camo-clad arm toward me. "Come on out of there."

As I tumble onto the leafy forest floor, sunlight hits my face and I gulp at the fresh air. I start crying, thankful I've lived to see another day.

Dani plops down in the clump of ferns that camouflage the door, crossbow at her side. "See? I told you I had your back, Tess."

37

We all troop back to the spa, where Dani brews a pot of organic chamomile tea. Detective Tucker doesn't rush to take her down to the station, and I realize he's giving us both a chance to get our bearings.

I call Thomas, Nikki Jo, and Charlotte, knowing they've been up all night praying for and looking for me. Thomas cries unabashedly into the phone, stirring my own tears. He leaves immediately to pick me up.

After a brief investigation of the mine, Detective Tucker reports on what they found. Mr. Daniel Seger had shielded himself in a minecart, which explains why my bullets ricocheted off metal. He sagged into the cart after Dani's crossbow bolt ripped directly between his eyes. He would have died instantly. One hand held a bow and the other held the arrow that was meant for me.

"This'll make the twelfth body for our poor coroner." Detective Tucker sips thoughtfully at his tea. Dani's remark about being tried by twelve instantly springs to mind.

Dani seems remarkably calm, a warm smile on her face as she prepares coffee for the officers. I lean toward Detective Tucker. "Is she going to be okay? I mean, she killed someone."

"She finally has closure," he says. "She sure made my job a lot easier. And she saved your life. She'll be okay."

Thomas bursts into the kitchen, his gaze bouncing around until he sees me. He rushes over and wraps me in a tight squeeze. Detective Tucker gives him a rundown on the situation. When Thomas finally lets go, he walks straight over to Dani. I worry that he might instruct the detective to cuff her, but instead he smiles and wraps her in a wordless hug.

Everything *is* going to be all right.

The need to see Mira Brooke overwhelms me, and I start to say my goodbyes. Dani apologizes for firing me. "The job is open if you ever want to come back," she says. "I owe you a lot for flushing Dad out of hiding."

Detective Tucker's beard tickles my head as I give him a final hug and thank you. As we walk out, he says, "Mrs. Spencer, you can call me Zeke."

Thomas gapes, his eyes wide. "Zeke," he whispers

near-reverently. "He told you to call him Zeke."

The Spencer family turns out in force for Thomas' swearing-in on Thursday. Thomas wears a tailored black suit, which makes him look like James Bond. I'm wearing my favorite dress. It has a mock-neck top covered with mint-colored pearls and a tulle skirt. I'm a bit overdressed but I feel like celebrating.

Mira Brooke takes her cues from us and claps when we do. Nikki Jo pulls numerous Kleenexes from her purse to quell the tears. Andrew grins, wearing an American flag T-shirt and dress pants for the occasion. Petey and Roger stand in typical Spencer-dude stances, with crossed arms and wide legs, proudly taking it all in.

Afterward, I hug Thomas. "Congrats to our new prosecuting attorney. You sure you don't mind if I miss your party?"

"It's just ice cream on the patio. Nothing big. I know Charlotte wanted to catch up with you before she has to move back to Morgantown."

Charlotte leaves next week to find an apartment and to settle in before the semester starts. I still can't believe she's going, and I doubt the Good Doctor can either. I find myself wishing he'd propose and keep her nearby. But Charlotte is a wandering spirit, a gypsy girl. I've always known that. She'll never stay in one place for long.

In Point Pleasant, I park the SUV and walk up Main Street to Kelly's Coffee. Even the creepy silver Mothman statue can't throw a damper on my mood...but I avoid looking at it anyway.

I'm surprised to find Rosemary sitting with Charlotte at an outdoor table. Rosemary stubs out her cigarette and smiles. "I hear you survived a run-in with a serial killer. That's no small feat."

"God protected me," I say.

"God and Dani," Charlotte says. "Boy, was there more to that California surfer girl than met the eye. I'm so glad she was there."

Rosemary grins. "And I've been keeping a check on Byron. Not because he's a killer, but because he's killer cute."

Charlotte groans. "He's half your age."

"And my dad's twice yours," she retorts.

"Not hardly." Charlotte sips at her café au lait and I order a cappuccino. Rosemary shrugs and lights another cigarette.

"Look at us," she says between puffs. "We solved this crime and busted a serial killer. It's like Nancy Drew, George, and Bess. I want to be Nancy."

Charlotte laughs. "You're not. More like Bess. You're just a sidekick."

Rosemary blows a little smoke cloud toward the sky, then stands. "I gotta get back to the bistro. Just remember I'm around if you ever need a little spy work done, *Nancy*." She winks at me.

Charlotte waves the waitress over and asks for a chocolate croissant. "I knew if I got one, Rosemary would eat half of it. Then again, you might eat half of it, but I don't mind."

As we eat and talk, shadows fall across our table. Charlotte glances up and I turn.

Axel stands with his employee, a petite girl who couldn't contrast with him more. "We were having our lunch food in town and saw you," he says. "Perhaps this is your friend?"

I nod. "Axel, this is Charlotte. Charlotte, Axel."

Charlotte offers him one of her huge, *you're-the-only-one-in-the-world* smiles. "Thank you for the flowers. I've never seen anything like them."

Axel isn't as moved as I thought he would be. Instead, he simply nods and turns to me. "You are safe? I have heard about this dead killer."

"Yes, I'm safe. Thanks for asking." I ramble on. "And thank you for telling me to see Miranda that day. I'm so glad I did."

If he knows what I'm talking about, he doesn't act like it. "I will be at the shop for a few weeks. Then I must do other business. Still you can find me there if you need me."

He nods and abruptly strides off, the tiny woman following in his wake like the ripple behind a boat.

Charlotte laughs. "So that's the mysterious Axel. He looks like...I don't know. Like the perfectly engineered man or something."

We sip our coffee and chat for another hour. All the while, I pretend like Charlotte isn't leaving me soon.

Back at home, Andrew just got the party started by pulling out Petey's old karaoke machine. He cranks up The Beach Boys and pretends to surf as he sings. Thomas holds Mira Brooke, who slurps at a half-melted ice-cream cone like it's the best thing on earth.

Thomas lays his hand on my leg. "It's a good day. You know what? For the first time in my life, I'm looking forward to going in to work."

"I know you are. And I'm so glad you're happy."

"I wouldn't be..." He chokes up. His hand slides up to my goose egg, which seems to have grown.

I try to lighten the mood. "First a black eye from my kid, then a lump on the head from a serial killer...hard to tell what's next."

"I know what's next." Crickets whir and night birds warble as he leans over and gives me a long kiss.

"We're going to enjoy life and you're going to stay away from trouble."

"Sounds like a plan."

When we finally wind down and walk back to our blissfully police-free cottage, Thomas offers to put Mira Brooke down for bed. I brew up some decaf, hoping to sit and enjoy a movie. But our home phone rings and there's no caller I.D. Most of the people I know call me on my cell.

When I pick up, a gravelly voice on the other end says, "Mrs. Spencer?"

"Yes, who's calling?"

"This is the Alderson Women's Prison. We have a Mrs. Pearletta Vee Lilly to speak to you."

My mother. "Yes, I'll take the call." I grit my teeth.

"Tessa honey, is that you?" Mom always yells into the phone like I can't hear. And given the happy lilt in her voice, I know something has changed.

"Momma, it's me. Why haven't you called or written? It's been a year!"

"Lots going on here. I been working hard. I knew you had your baby and I didn't want to put extra pressure on you. But now I gotta tell you. I'm getting out in three months! And I'll need a place to stay."

So much for avoiding trouble. Once again, trouble has found me.

COUSIN NELMA'S BANANA PUDDING

INGREDIENTS:
-3 regular or 2 large instant vanilla puddings
-5 cups milk
-1 large carton Cool Whip
-box vanilla wafers
-bunch of firm bananas

Mix pudding and milk together and then fold in one large carton Cool Whip. Layer 5 or 6 cut-up bananas with the Cool Whip mix, top with vanilla wafers. Repeat the layers. Put a layer of Cool Whip mix and vanilla wafer crumbs on top. Chill in refrigerator. Layers look amazing in a clear glass bowl.

ABOUT THE AUTHOR

 **HEATHER DAY GILBERT** enjoys writing stories about authentic, believable marriages. Born and raised in the West Virginia mountains, she believes that bittersweet, generational stories are in her blood. A graduate of Bob Jones University, Heather has been married for eighteen years and has three children.

Heather's Viking historical novel, *God's Daughter*, was an Amazon Norse Bestseller for an entire year. She is also the author of *Miranda Warning*, Book One in *A Murder in the Mountains* Series, and the *Indie Publishing Handbook: Four Key Elements for the Self-Publisher*.

ONLINE:

Website: http://heatherdaygilbert.com

Facebook Author Page:

https://www.facebook.com/heatherdaygilbert

Twitter: @heatherdgilbert

Pinterest: https://www.pinterest.com/heatherdgilbert/

Goodreads:

https://www.goodreads.com/author/show/7232683.Hea

ther_Day_Gilbert

E-Mail: heatherdaygilbert@gmail.com

FOR NEWS ON UPCOMING RELEASES, FOLLOW HEATHER'S NEWSLETTER HERE:

http://heatherdaygilbert.com/newsletter-signup/

FIND SAMPLE CHAPTERS HERE:

GOD'S DAUGHTER—
http://bit.ly/1yy5NRH

MIRANDA WARNING—
http://bit.ly/1zn77lw

Thank you for reading **Trial by Twelve.** If you enjoyed this book, please take time to leave a review on **Amazon** or **Goodreads**. Encouraging words feed an author's soul!

47213680R00158

Made in the USA
Lexington, KY
01 December 2015